ROBERT WILSON

Robert Wilson was born in 1957. A graduate of Oxford University, he has worked in shipping and advertising in London and trading in West Africa. He is married and divides his time between England, Spain and Portugal.

He was awarded the CWA Gold Dagger for Fiction for his fifth novel, *A Small Death in Lisbon*.

ROBERT WILSON

The Hidden Assassins

HARPER

Harper
An imprint of HarperCollins*Publishers*
77–85 Fulham Palace Road,
Hammersmith, London W6 8JB

www.harpercollins.co.uk

This paperback edition 2007
2

First published in Great Britain by
HarperCollins*Publishers* 2006

ISBN-13: 978 0 00 732212 1

FSC is a non-profit international organisation established to promote the
responsible management of the world's forests. Products carrying the FSC
label are independently certified to assure consumers that they come
from forests that are managed to meet the social, economic and
ecological needs of present and future generations.

Find out more about HarperCollins and the environment at
www.harpercollins.co.uk/green

For Jane and my mother
and
Bindy, Simon and Abigail

ACKNOWLEDGEMENTS

This book would have been impossible without extensive research in Morocco, especially to see how all levels of Moroccan society are reacting to the friction between Islam and the West. I would like to thank Laila for her hospitality and for introducing me to people from all walks of life. They gave me valuable insights into the Arab world's point of view. I must stress that although all opinions are faithfully represented, none of the characters in this book remotely resembles any real person, alive or dead. They are all figments of my imagination and were generated to perform their functions in my story.

As always, I would like to thank my friends Mick Lawson and José Manuel Blanco for putting me up and putting up with me. They made the Seville end of my research for this book a lot easier. My thanks to the Linc language school in Seville and my teacher Lourdes Martinez, for doing her best to improve my Spanish.

I have been published by HarperCollins for just over ten years and I think it fitting that after a decade of hard work on my behalf I should thank my editor, Julia Wisdom, who has not only offered perceptive advice about my books and brought them successfully to the market place, but has also been one of my greatest in-house proponents.

Finally I would like to thank my wife, Jane, who has helped me with my research, spurred me on through the long months of writing, and been my first, and unflagging, reader and critic. Some think that being a writer is hard, but spare a thought for the writer's wife, who while working and supporting has to watch much writhing and torment and is rewarded with scant praise and little compensation for the horrors she must witness. You'd only do it for love and I thank her for it and return it doubled.

Turning and turning in the widening gyre
The falcon cannot hear the falconer;
Things fall apart; the centre cannot hold;
Mere anarchy is loosed upon the world,
The blood-dimmed tide is loosed, and everywhere
The ceremony of innocence is drowned;
The best lack all conviction, while the worst
Are full of passionate intensity.

'The Second Coming' W.B. YEATS

And now, what will become of us without the barbarians?
Those people were a kind of solution.

'Waiting for the Barbarians' CONSTANTINE CAVAFY

The West End, London – Thursday, 9th March 2006

'So, how's your new job going?' asked Najib.

'I work for this woman,' said Mouna. 'She's called Amanda Turner. She's not even thirty and she's already an account director. You know what I do for her? I book her holidays. That's what I've been doing all week.'

'Is she going somewhere nice?'

Mouna laughed. She loved Najib. He was so quiet and not of this world. Meeting him was like coming across a *palmerie* in the desert.

'Can you believe this?' she said. 'She's going on a pilgrimage.'

'I didn't know English people went on pilgrimages.'

Mouna was, in fact, very impressed by Amanda Turner, but she was much keener to receive Najib's approbation.

'Well, it's not exactly religious. I mean, the reason she's going isn't.'

'Where is this pilgrimage?'

'It's in Spain near Seville. It's called La Romería del Rocío,' said Mouna. 'Every year people from all over

1

Andalucía gather together in this little village called El Rocío. On something called the Pentecost Monday, they bring out the Virgin from the church and everybody goes wild, dancing and feasting, as far as I can tell.'

'I don't get it,' said Najib.

'Nor do I. But I can tell you the reason Amanda's going is not for the parading of the Virgin,' said Mouna. 'She's going because it's one big party for four days – drinking, dancing, singing – you know what English people are like.'

Najib nodded. He knew what they were like.

'So why has it taken you all week?' he asked.

'Because the whole of Seville is completely booked up and Amanda has loads, I mean loads, of requirements. The four rooms have all got to be together . . .'

'Four rooms?'

'She's going with her boyfriend, Jim "Fat Cat" Maitland,' said Mouna. 'Then there's her sister and *her* boyfriend and two other couples. The guys all work in the same company as Jim – Kraus, Maitland, Powers.'

'What does Jim do in his company?'

'It's a hedge fund. Don't ask me what that means,' said Mouna. 'All I know is that it's in the building they call the Gherkin and . . . guess how much money he made last year?'

Najib shook his head. He made very little money. So little it wasn't important to him.

'Eight million pounds?' said Mouna, dangling it as a question.

'How much did you say?'

'I know. You can't believe it, can you? The lowest paid guy in Jim's company made five million last year.'

'I can see why they would have a lot of requirements,' said Najib, sipping his black tea.

'The rooms have all got to be together. They want to stay a night before the pilgrimage, and then three nights after, and then a night in Granada, and then come back to Seville for another two nights. And there's got to be a garage, because Jim won't park his Porsche Cayenne in the street,' said Mouna. 'Do you know what a Porsche Cayenne is, Najib?'

'A car?' said Najib, scratching himself through his beard.

'I'll tell you what Amanda calls it: Jim's Big Fuck Off to Global Warming.'

Najib winced at her language and she wished she hadn't been so eager to impress.

'It's a four-wheel drive,' said Mouna, quickly, 'which goes a hundred and fifty-*six* miles an hour. Amanda says you can watch the fuel gauge going down when Jim hits a hundred. And you know, they're taking four cars. They could easily fit in two, but they have to take four. I mean, these people, Najib, you cannot believe it.'

'Oh, I think I can, Mouna,' said Najib. 'I think I can.'

The City of London – Thursday, 23rd March 2006

He stood across the street from the entrance to the underground car park. His face was indiscernible beyond the greasy, fake fur-lined rim of the green parka's hood. He walked backwards and forwards, hands shoved deep down into his pockets. One of his trainers was coming apart and the lace of the other dragged and flapped about the sodden frayed bottom of his faded jeans, which seemed to suck on the wet pavement. He was muttering.

He could have been any one of the hundreds of unseen people drawn to the city to live at ankle height in underground passages, to scuff around on cardboard sheets in shop doorways, to drift like lost souls in the limbo of purgatory amongst the living and the visible, with their real lives and jobs and credit on their cards and futures in every conceivable commodity, including time.

Except that he *was* being seen, as we are all being seen, as we have all become walkers-on with bit parts in the endlessly tedious movie of everyday life. Often in the early mornings he was the star of this grainy black-and-white documentary, with barely an extra in sight and only the sporty traffic of the early traders and Far East fund managers providing any action. Later, as the sandwich shops opened and the streets filled with bankers, brokers and analysts, his role reverted to 'local colour' and he would often be lost in the date or the flickering numbers of time running past.

Like all CCTV actors, his talent was completely missable, his Reality TV potential would remain undiscovered unless, for some reason, it was perceived that his part was crucial, and the editor of everyday life suddenly realized that he had occupied the moment when the little girl was last seen, or the young lad was led away or, as so often happens in the movies, briefcases were exchanged.

There was none of that excitement here.

The solitary male or female (under the hood not even that was clear) moved in the tide of extras, sometimes with them, sometimes against. He was extra to the extras and, worse than superfluous, he was getting in the way. He did this for hour after hour, week after week, month after . . . He was only there for a month. For four weeks he muttered and shuffled across the cracks in the pavement opposite the underground car park and then he was gone. Reality TV rolled on without him, without ever realizing that a star of the silent screen had been in its eye for just over 360 hours.

Had there been a soundtrack it would not have helped. Even if a mike had been placed within the horrible greasy hood of the parka it would have clarified nothing. All that would have registered was the mutterings of a marginalized moron, telling himself the colour, model and registration number of apparently random cars and the time they passed his patch of pavement. It was surely the obsessive work of a lunatic.

What sort of sophisticated surveillance equipment would have been able to pick up that the eyes deep inside the darkness of the hood were only choosing cars that went into the underground car park of the building across the street? And even if there was equipment that could have made that connection, would it also have been able to discover that the stream of uninteresting data was being recorded on to the hard disk of a palm-sized dictaphone in the inside pocket of the parka?

Only then would the significance of this superfluous human being have been realized and the editor of everyday life, if he was being attentive that morning, might have sat up in his chair and thought: Here we have a star in the making.

1

Dead bodies are never pretty. Even the most talented undertaker with a genius for *maquillage* cannot bring the animation of life back to a corpse. But some dead bodies are uglier than others. They have been taken over by another life form. Bacteria have turned their juices and excretions into noxious gas, which slithers along the body's cavities and under the skin, until it's drum tight over the corruption within. The stench is so powerful it enters the central nervous system of the living and their revulsion reaches beyond the perimeter of their being. They become edgy. It's best not to stand too close to people around a 'bloater'.

Normally Inspector Jefe Javier Falcón had a mantra, which he played in the back of his mind when confronted by this sort of corpse. He could stomach all manner of violence done to bodies – gunshot craters, knife gashes, bludgeon dents, strangulation bruises, poisoned pallor – but this transformation by corruption, the bloat and stink, had recently begun to disturb him. He thought it might just be the psychology of decadence, the mind troubled by the slide to the only

7

possible end of age; except that this wasn't the ordinary decay of death. It was to do with the corruption of the body – the heat's rapid transformation of a slim girl into a stout middle-aged matron or, as in the case of this body that they were excavating from the rubbish of the landfill site beyond the outskirts of the city, the metamorphosis of an ordinary man to the taut girth of a sumo wrestler.

The body had stiffened with rigor mortis and had come to rest in the most degrading position. Worse than a defeated sumo wrestler tipped from the ring to land head first in the front row of the baying crowd, his modesty protected by the thick strap of his *mawashi*, this man was naked. Had he been clothed he might have been kneeling as a Muslim supplicant (his head even pointed east), but he wasn't. And so he looked like someone preparing himself for bestial violation, his face pressed into the bed of decay underneath him, as if unable to bear the shame of this ultimate defilement.

As he took in the scene Falcón realized that he wasn't playing his usual mantra and that his mind was occupied by what had happened to him as he'd taken the call alerting him to the discovery of the body. To escape the noise in the café where he'd been drinking his café solo, he'd backed out through the door and collided with a woman. They'd said 'Perdón', exchanged a startled look and then been transfixed. The woman was Consuelo Jiménez. In the four years since their affair Falcón had only had a glimpse of her four or five times in crowded streets or shops and now he'd bumped into her. They said nothing. She didn't go into the café after all, but disappeared quickly back into the stream of shoppers. She had, however, left her imprint on him and the closed shrine in his mind devoted to her had been reopened.

Earlier the Médico Forense had stepped carefully through the rubbish to confirm that the man was dead. Now the forensics were concluding their work, bagging anything of interest and removing it from the scene. The Médico Forense, still masked up and dressed in a white boiler suit, paid his second visit to the victim. His eyes searched and narrowed at what they found. He made notes and walked over to where Falcón was standing with the duty judge, Juez Juan Romero.

'I can't see any obvious cause of death,' he said. 'He didn't die from having his hands cut off. That was done afterwards. His wrists have been very tightly tourniqueted. There are no contusions around the neck and no bullet holes or knife wounds. He's been scalped and I can't see any catastrophic damage to the skull. He might have been poisoned, but I can't tell from his face, which has been burnt off with acid. Time of death looks to be around forty-eight hours ago.'

Juez Romero's dark brown eyes blinked over his face mask at each devastating revelation. He hadn't handled a murder investigation for more than two years and he wasn't used to this level of brutality in the few murders that had come his way.

'They didn't want him recognized, did they?' said Falcón. 'Any distinguishing marks on the rest of the body?'

'Let me get him back to the lab and cleaned up. He's covered in filth.'

'What about other body damage?' asked Falcón. 'He must have arrived in the back of a refuse truck to end up here. There should be some marks.'

'Not that I can see. There might be abrasions under the filth and I'll pick up any fractures and ruptured organs back at the Forensic Institute once I've opened him up.'

Falcón nodded. Juez Romero signed off the *levantamiento del cadáver* and the paramedics moved in and thought about how they were going to manipulate a stiffened corpse in this position into a body bag and on to the stretcher. Farce crept into the tragedy of the scene. They wanted to cause as little disturbance as possible to the body's noxious gases. In the end they opened up the body bag on the stretcher and lifted him, still prostrate, and placed him on top. They tucked his wrist stumps and feet into the bag and zipped it up over his raised buttocks. They carried the tented structure to the ambulance, watched by a gang of municipal workers, who'd gathered to see the last moments of the drama. They all laughed and turned away as one of their number said something about 'taking it up the arse for eternity'.

Tragedy, farce and now vulgarity, thought Falcón.

The forensics completed their search of the area immediately around the body and brought their bagged exhibits over to Falcón.

'We've got some addresses on envelopes found close to the body,' said Felipe. 'Three have got the same street names. It should help you to find where he was dumped. We reckon that's how he ended up in that body position, from lying foetally in the bottom of a bin.'

'We're also pretty sure he was wrapped in this –' said Jorge, holding up a large plastic bag stuffed with a grimy white sheet. 'There's traces of blood from his severed hands. We'll match it up later . . .'

'He was naked when I first saw him,' said Falcón.

'There was some loose stitching which we assume got ripped open in the refuse truck,' said Jorge. 'The sheet was snagged on one of the stumps of his wrists.'

'The Médico Forense said the wrists were well tourniqueted and the hands removed after death.'

'They were neatly severed, too,' said Jorge. 'No hack job – surgical precision.'

'Any decent butcher could have done it,' said Felipe. 'But the face burnt off with acid *and* scalped . . . What do you make of that, Inspector Jefe?'

'There must have been something special about him, to go to that trouble,' said Falcón. 'What's in the bin liner?'

'Some gardening detritus,' said Jorge. 'We think it had been dumped in the bin to cover the body.'

'We're going to do a wider search of the area now,' said Felipe. 'Pérez spoke to the guy operating the digger, who found the body, and there was some talk of a black plastic sheet. They might have done their post-mortem surgery on it, sewed him up in the shroud, wrapped him in the plastic and then dumped him.'

'And you know how much we love black plastic for prints,' said Jorge.

Falcón noted the addresses on the envelopes and they split up. He went back to his car, stripping off his face mask. His olfactory organ hadn't tired sufficiently for the stink of urban waste not to lodge itself in his throat. The insistent grinding of the diggers drowned out the cawing of the scavenging birds, wheeling darkly against the white sky. This was a sad place even for an insentient corpse to end up.

Sub-Inspector Emilio Pérez was sitting on the back

of a patrol car chatting to another member of the homicide squad, the ex-nun Cristina Ferrera. Pérez, who was well built with the dark good looks of a 1930s matinée idol, seemed to be of a different species to the small, blonde and rather plain young woman who'd joined the homicide squad from Cádiz four years ago. But, whereas Pérez had a tendency to be bovine in both demeanour and mentality, Ferrera was quick, intuitive and unrelenting. Falcón gave them the addresses from the envelopes, listing the questions he wanted asked, and Ferrera repeated them back before he could finish.

'They sewed him into a shroud,' he said to Cristina Ferrera as she went for the car. 'They carefully removed his hands, burnt his face off, scalped him, but sewed him into a shroud.'

'I suppose they think they've shown him some sort of respect,' said Ferrera. 'Like they do at sea, or for burial in mass graves after a disaster.'

'Respect,' said Falcón. 'Right after they've shown him the ultimate disrespect by taking his life and his identity. There's something ritualistic and ruthless about this, don't you think?'

'Perhaps they were religious,' said Ferrera, raising an ironic eyebrow. 'You know, a lot of terrible things have been done in God's name, Inspector Jefe.'

Falcón drove back into the centre of Seville in strange yellowing light as a huge storm cloud, which had been gathering over the Sierra de Aracena, began to encroach on the city from the northwest. The radio told him that there would be an evening of heavy rain. It was probably going to be the last rain before the long hot summer.

At first he thought that it might be the physical and mental jolt he'd had from colliding with Consuelo that morning which was making him feel anxious. Or was it the change in the atmospheric pressure, or some residual edginess left from seeing the bloated corpse on the dump? As he sat at the traffic lights he realized that it ran deeper than all that. His instinct was telling him that this was the end of an old order and the ominous start of something new. The unidentifiable corpse was like a neurosis; an ugly protrusion prodding the consciousness of the city from a greater horror underneath. It was the sense of that greater horror, with its potential to turn minds, move spirits and change lives that he was finding so disturbing.

By the time he arrived back at the Jefatura, after a series of meetings with judges in the Edificio de los Juzgados, it was seven o'clock and evening seemed to have come early. The smell of rain was as heavy as metal in the ionized air. The thunder still seemed to be a long way off, but the sky was darkening to a premature night and flashes of lightning startled, like death just missed.

Pérez and Ferrera were waiting for him in his office. Their eyes followed him as he went to the window and the first heavy drops of rain rapped against the glass. Contentment was a strange human state, he thought, as a light steam rose from the car park. Just at the moment life seemed boring and the desire for change emerged like a brilliant idea, along came a new, sinister vitality and the mind was suddenly scrambling back to what appeared to be prelapsarian bliss.

'What have you got?' he asked, moving along the window to his desk and collapsing in the chair.

'You didn't give us a time of death,' said Ferrera.

'Sorry. Forty-eight hours was the estimate.'

'We found the bins where the envelopes were dumped. They're in the old city centre, on the corner of a cul-de-sac and Calle Boteros, between the Plaza de la Alfalfa and the Plaza Cristo de Burgos.'

'When do they empty those bins?'

'Every night between eleven and midnight,' said Pérez.

'So if, as the Médico Forense says, he died some time in the evening of Saturday 3rd June,' said Ferrera, 'they probably wouldn't have been able to dump the body until three in the morning on Sunday.'

'Where are those bins now?'

'We've had them sent down to forensics to test for blood traces.'

'But we might be out of luck there,' said Pérez. 'Felipe and Jorge have found some black plastic sheeting, which they think was wrapped around the body.'

'Did any of the people you spoke to at the addresses on the envelopes remember seeing any black plastic sheeting in the bottom of one of the bins?'

'We didn't know about the black plastic sheeting when we interviewed them.'

'Of course you didn't,' said Falcón, his brain not concentrated on the details, still drifting about in his earlier unease. 'Why do you think the body was dumped at three in the morning?'

'Saturday night near the Alfalfa . . . you know what it's like around there . . . all the kids in the bars and out on the streets.'

'Why choose those bins, if it's so busy?'

'Maybe they know those bins,' said Pérez. 'They knew

that they could park down a dark, quiet cul-de-sac and what the collection times were. They could plan. Dumping the body would only take a few seconds.'

'Any apartments overlooking the bins?'

'We'll go around the apartments in the cul-de-sac again tomorrow,' said Pérez. 'The apartment with the best view is at the end, but there was nobody at home.'

A long, pulsating flash of lightning was accompanied by a clap of thunder so loud that it seemed to crack open the sky above their heads. They all instinctively ducked and the Jefatura was plunged into darkness. They fumbled around for a torch, while the rain thrashed against the building and drove in waves across the car park. Ferrera propped a flashlight up against some files and they sat back. More lightning left them blinking, with the window frame burnt on to their retinae. The emergency generators started up in the basement. The lights flickered back on. Falcón's mobile vibrated on the desktop: a text from the Médico Forense telling him that the autopsy had been completed and he would be free from 8.30 a.m. to discuss it. Falcón sent a text back agreeing to see him first thing. He flung the mobile back on the desk and stared into the wall.

'You seem a little uneasy, Inspector Jefe,' said Pérez, who had a habit of stating the obvious, while Falcón had a habit of ignoring him.

'We have an unidentified corpse, which could prove to be unidentifiable,' said Falcón, marshalling his thoughts, trying to give Pérez and Ferrera a focus for their investigative work. 'How many people do you think were involved in this murder?'

'A minimum of two,' said Ferrera.

'Killing, scalping, severing hands, burning off features

15

with acid . . . yes, why did they cut off his hands when they could have easily burnt off his prints with acid?'

'Something significant about his hands,' said Pérez.

Falcón and Ferrera exchanged a look.

'Keep thinking, Emilio,' said Falcón. 'Anyway, it was planned and premeditated and it was important that his identity was not known. Why?'

'Because the identity of the corpse will point to the killers,' said Pérez. 'Most victims are killed by people –'

'Or?' said Falcón. 'If there was no *obvious* link?'

'The identity of the victim and/or knowledge of his skills might jeopardize a future operation,' said Ferrera.

'Good. Now tell me how many people you really think it took to dispose of that body in one of those bins,' said Falcón. 'They're chest high to a normal person and the whole thing has got to be done in seconds.'

'Three to deal with the body and two for lookout,' said Pérez.

'If you tipped the bin over to the edge of the car boot it could be done with two men,' said Ferrera. 'Anybody coming down Calle Boteros at that time would be drunk and shouting. You might need a driver in the car. Three maximum.'

'Three or five, what does that tell you?'

'It's a gang,' said Pérez.

'Doing what?'

'Drugs?' he said. 'Cutting off his hands, burning off his face . . .'

'Drug runners don't normally sew people into shrouds,' said Falcón. 'They tend to shoot people and there was no bullet hole . . . not even a knife wound.'

'It didn't seem like an execution,' said Ferrera, 'more like a regrettable necessity.'

16

Falcón told them they were to revisit all the apartments overlooking the bins first thing in the morning before everybody went to work. They were to establish if there was black plastic sheeting in any of the bins and if a car was seen or heard at around three in the morning on Sunday.

Down in the forensic lab, Felipe and Jorge had the tables pushed back and the black plastic sheet laid out on the floor. The two large bins from Calle Boteros were already in the corner, taped shut. Jorge was at a microscope while Felipe was on all fours on the plastic sheet, wearing his custom-made magnifying spectacles.

'We've got a blood group match from the victim to the white shroud and to the black plastic sheet. We hope to have a DNA match by tomorrow morning,' said Jorge. 'It looks to me as if they put him face down on the plastic to do the surgery.' He gave Falcón the measurements between a saliva deposit and some blood deposits and two pubic hairs which all conformed to the victim's height.

'We're running DNA tests on those, too,' he said.

'What about the acid on the face?'

'That must have been done elsewhere and rinsed off. There's no sign of it.'

'Any prints?'

'No fingerprints, just a footprint in the top left quadrant,' said Felipe. 'Jorge has matched it to a Nike trainer, as worn by thousands of people.'

'Are you going to be able to look at those bins tonight?'

'We'll take a look, but if he was well wrapped up I don't hold out much hope for blood or saliva,' said Felipe.

17

'Have you run a check on missing persons?' asked Jorge.

'We don't even know if he was Spanish yet,' said Falcón. 'I'm seeing the Médico Forense tomorrow morning. Let's hope there are some distinguishing marks.'

'His pubic hair was dark,' said Jorge, grinning. 'And his blood group was O positive . . . if that's any help?'

'Keep up the brilliant work,' said Falcón.

It was still raining, but in a discouragingly sensible way after the reckless madness of the initial downpour. Falcón did some paperwork with his mind elsewhere. He turned away from his computer and stared at the reflection of his office in the dark window. The fluorescent light shivered. Pellets of rain drummed against the glass as if a lunatic wanted to attract his attention. Falcón was surprised at himself. He'd been such a scientific investigator in the past, always keen to get his hands on autopsy reports and forensic evidence. Now he spent more time tuning in to his intuition. He tried to persuade himself that it was experience but sometimes it seemed like laziness. A buzz from his mobile jolted him: a text from his current girlfriend, Laura, inviting him to dinner. He looked down at the screen and found himself unconsciously rubbing the arm which had made contact with Consuelo's body in the entrance of the café. He hesitated as he reached for the mobile to reply. Why, suddenly, was everything so much more complicated? He'd wait until he got back home.

The traffic was slow in the rain. The radio news commented on the successful parading of the Virgin of Rocío, which had taken place that day. Falcón crossed the river and joined the metal snake heading north. He sat at the traffic lights and scribbled a note without thinking before filtering right down Calle Reyes Católicos. From there he drove into the maze of streets where he lived in the massive, rambling house he'd inherited six years ago. He parked up between the orange trees that led to the entrance of the house on Calle Bailén but didn't get out. He was wrestling with his uneasiness again and this time it was to do with Consuelo – what he'd seen in her face that morning. They'd both been startled, but it hadn't just been shock that had registered in her eyes. It was anguish.

He got out of the car, opened the smaller door within the brass-studded oak portal and went through to the patio, where the marble flags still glistened from the rain. A blinking light beyond the glass door to his study told him that he had two phone messages. He hit the button and stood in the dark looking out through the cloister at the bronze running boy in the fountain. The voice of his Moroccan friend, Yacoub Diouri, filled the room. He greeted Javier in Arabic and then slipped into perfect Spanish. He was flying to Madrid on his way to Paris next weekend and wondered if they could meet up. Was that coincidence or synchronicity? The only reason he'd met Yacoub Diouri, one of the few men he'd become close to, was because of Consuelo Jiménez. That was the thing about intuition, you began to believe that everything had significance.

The second message was from Laura, who still wanted to know if he would be coming for dinner that night; it would be just the two of them. He smiled at that. His relationship with Laura was not exclusive. She had other male companions she saw regularly and that had suited him . . . until now when, for no apparent reason, it was different. Paella and spending the night with Laura suddenly seemed ridiculous.

He called her and said that he wouldn't be able to make dinner but that he would drop by for a drink later.

There was no food in the house. His housekeeper had assumed he would go out for dinner. He hadn't eaten all day. The body on the dump had interrupted his lunch plans and ruined his appetite. Now he was hungry. He went for a walk. The streets were fresh after the rain and full of people. He didn't really start thinking where he was going until he found himself heading round the back of the Omnium Sanctorum church. Only then did he admit that he was going to eat at Consuelo's new restaurant.

The waiter brought him a menu and he ordered immediately. The pan de casa arrived quickly; thinly sliced ham sitting on a spread of salmorejo on toast. He enjoyed it with a beer. Feeling suddenly bold he took out one of his cards and wrote on the back: *I am eating here and wondered if you would join me for a glass of wine. Javier.* When the waiter came back with the revuelto de setas, scrambled eggs and mushrooms, he poured a glass of red rioja and Javier gave him the card.

Later the waiter returned with some tiny lamb chops and topped up his glass of wine.

'She's not in,' he said. 'I've left the card on her desk so that she knows you were here.'

Falcón knew he was lying. It was one of the few advantages of being a detective. He ate the chops feeling privately foolish that he'd believed in the synchronicity of the moment. He sipped at his third glass of wine and ordered coffee. By 10.40 p.m. he was out in the street again. He leaned against the wall opposite the entrance to the restaurant, thinking that he might catch her on the way out.

As he stood there waiting patiently he covered a lot of ground in his head. It was amazing how little thought he'd given to his inner life since he'd stopped seeing his shrink four years ago.

And when, an hour later, he gave up his vigil he knew precisely what he was going to do. He was determined to finish his superficial relationship with Laura and, if his world of work would let him, he would devote himself to bringing Consuelo back into his life.

2

Consuelo Jiménez was sitting in the office of her flag-
ship restaurant, in the heart of La Macarena, the old
working-class neighbourhood of Seville. She was in a
state of heightened anxiety and the three heavy shots
of The Macallan, which she'd taken to drinking at this
time of night, were doing nothing to alleviate it. Her
state had not been improved by bumping into Javier
early in the day and it had been made worse by the
knowledge that he'd been eating his dinner barely ten
metres from where she was now sitting. His card lay
on the desk in front of her.

She was in possession of a terrible clarity about her
mental and physical state. She was not somebody who,
having fallen into a trough of despair, lost control of
her life and plunged unconsciously into an orgy of
self-destruction. She was more meticulous than that,
more detached. So detached that at times she'd found
herself looking down on her own blonde head as the
mind beneath stumbled about in the wreckage of her
inner life. It was a very strange state to be in: physically in good shape for her age, mentally still very

22

focused on her business, beautifully turned out as always, but . . . how to put this? She had no words for what was happening inside her. All she had to describe it was an image from a TV documentary on global warming: vital elements of an ancient glacier's primitive structure had melted in some unusually fierce summer heat and, without warning, a vast tonnage of ice had collapsed in a protracted roar into a lake below. She knew, from the ghastly plummet in her own organs, that she was watching a pre-figurement of what might happen to her unless she did something fast.

The whisky glass travelled to her mouth and back to the desk, transported by a hand that she did not feel belonged to her. She was grateful for the ethereal sting of the alcohol because it reminded her that she was still sentient. She was playing with a business card, turning it over and over, rubbing the embossed name and profession with her thumb. Her manager knocked and came in.

'We're finished now,' he said. 'We'll be locking up in five minutes. There's nothing left to do here . . . you should go home.'

'That man who was here earlier, one of the waiters said he was outside. Are you sure he's gone?'

'I'm sure,' said the manager.

'I'll let myself out of the side door,' she said, giving him one of her hard, professional looks.

He backed off. Consuelo was sorry. He was a good man, who knew when a person needed help and also when that help was unacceptable. What was going on inside Consuelo was too personal to be sorted out in an after-hours chat between proprietor and manager.

This wasn't about unpaid bills or difficult clients. This was about . . . everything.

She went back to the card. It belonged to a clinical psychologist called Alicia Aguado. Over the last eighteen months Consuelo had made six appointments with this woman and failed to turn up for any of them. She'd given a different name each time she'd made these appointments, but Alicia Aguado had recognized her voice from the first call. Of course she would. She was blind, and the blind develop other senses. On the last two occasions Alicia Aguado had said: 'If ever you *have* to see me, you must call. I will fit you in whenever – early morning or late at night. You must realize that I am always here when you need me.' That had shocked Consuelo. Alicia Aguado knew. Even Consuelo's iciest professional tone had betrayed her need for help.

The hand reached for the bottle and refilled the glass. The whisky vaporized into her mind. She also knew why she wanted to see this particular psychologist: Alicia Aguado had treated Javier Falcón. When she'd run into him in the street, it had been like a reminder. But a reminder of what? The 'fling' she'd had with him? She only called it a fling because that's what it looked like from the outside – some days of dinners and wild sex. But she'd broken it off because . . . She writhed in her chair at the memory. What reason had she given him? Because she was hopeless when in love? She turned into somebody else when she got into a relationship? Whatever it was, she'd invented some-thing unanswerable, refused to see him or answer his calls. And now he was back like an extra motivation.

She hadn't been able to ignore a recent and more worrying psychological development, which had started to occur in the brief moments when she wasn't working with her usual fierce, almost manic, drive. When distracted or tired at the end of the day sex would come into her mind, but like a midnight intruder. She imagined herself having new and vital affairs with strangers. Her fantasies drifted towards rough, possibly dangerous men and assumed pornographic dimensions, with herself at the centre of almost unimaginable goings on. She'd always hated porn, had found it both disgustingly biological and boring, but now, however much she tried to fight it with her intelligence, she was aware of her arousal: saliva in her mouth, the constriction of her throat. And it was happening again, now, even with her mind apparently engaged. She kicked back her chair, tossed Aguado's card into the gaping hole of her handbag, lunged at her cigarettes, lit up and paced the office floor, smoking too fast and hard.

These imaginings disgusted her. Why was she thinking about such trash? Why not think about her children? Her three darling boys – Ricardo, Matías and Darío – asleep at home in the care of a nanny. In the care of a nanny! She had promised that she would never do that. After Raúl, her husband, their father, had been murdered she had been determined to give them all her attention so that they would never feel the lack of a parent. And look at her now – thinking of fucking while they were at home in another person's care. She didn't deserve to be a mother. She tore her handbag off the desk. Javier's card fluttered to the floor.

She wanted to be out in the open, breathing the rain-rinsed air. The five or six shots of The Macallan she'd drunk meant that she had to walk up to the Basilica Macarena to get a taxi. To do this she had to pass the

Plaza del Pumarejo, where a bunch of drunks and addicts hung out all day, every day, and well into the night. The plaza, under a canopy of trees still dripping from the earlier storm, had a raised platform with a closed kiosk at one end and at the other, near the shuttered Bodega de Gamacho, a group of a dozen or so burnt-out cases.

The air was cool around Consuelo's bare legs, which were numbed by the whisky. She had not considered how obtrusive her peach-coloured satin suit would be under the street lamps. She walked behind the kiosk and along the pavement by the old Palacio del Pumarejo. Some of the group were standing and boozing, gathered around a man who was talking, while others slumped on benches in a stupor.

The wiry central figure in a black shirt open to the waist was familiar to Consuelo. His talk to this unsavoury audience was more of an oration, because he had a politician's way with words. He had long black hair, eyebrows angled sharply into his nose and a lean, hard, pockmarked face. She knew why the group around him hung on his words and it had nothing to do with the content. It was because under those satanic eyebrows he had very bright, light green eyes, which stared out of his dark face, alarming whoever they settled on. They gave the powerful impression of a man who had quick access to a blade. He drank from a bottle of cheap wine, which hung by his side with his fore-finger plugged into its neck.

A month ago, while Consuelo was waiting to cross the road at a traffic light, he'd approached her from behind and muttered words of such obscenity that they'd entered her mind like a shiv. Consuelo had remonstrated loudly when it happened. But, unlike the usual perpetrators, who would slink off into the crowds of shoppers, ignoring her, he'd got up close and silenced her with those green eyes and a quick wink, that made her think he knew something about her that she, herself, did not.

'I know your sort,' he'd said, and touched the corner of his mouth with the point of his tongue.

His bravado had paralysed her vocal cords. That and the horrible little kiss he'd blown her, which found its way to her neck like a horsefly.

Consuelo, distracted by these memories, had slowed to a halt. A member of the group spotted her and jerked his head in her direction. The orator stepped towards the railing holding the bottle up, letting it dangle from his forefinger.

'Fancy a drink?' he said. 'We haven't got any glasses, but I'll let you suck it off my finger if you want.'

A low, gurgling laugh came from the group, which included some women. Startled, Consuelo began walking again. The man jumped off the raised platform. The steel tips on the heels of his boots hammered the cobbles. He blocked her path and started to dance an extremely suggestive Sevillana, with much pelvic thrusting. The group backed him up with some flamenco clapping.

'Come on, Doña Consuelo,' he said. 'Let's see you move. You look as if you've got a decent pair of legs on you.'

She was shocked to hear him use her name. Terror slashed through her insides, tugging something strangely exciting behind it. Muscles quivered in the backs of her thighs. Disparate thoughts barged into each other in her mind. Why the hell had she put herself in such a position? She wondered how rough his hands would be. He looked strong – potentially violent.

The sheer perversity of these thoughts jolted her back to the reality. She had to get away from him. She veered off down a side street, walking as fast as her kitten heels would permit on the cobbles. He was behind her, steel tips leisurely clicking.

'Fucking hell, Doña Consuelo, I only asked you for a dance,' he shouted after her, a mocking inflexion on her title. 'Now you're leading me astray down this dark alley. For God's sake, have some self-respect, woman. Don't go showing your eagerness so early on. We've barely met, we haven't even danced.'

Consuelo kept going, breathing fast. All she had to do was get to the end of the street, turn left and she'd be at the gates of the old city and there would be traffic and people . . . a taxi back to her real life at home in Santa Clara. An alley appeared on her left, she saw the lights of the main road through the buildings leaning into each other. She darted down it. Shit, the cobbles were wet and all over the place. It was too dark and her heels were slipping. She wanted to scream when his hand finally landed on her shoulder, but it was like in those dreams where the need to yell the neighbourhood awake produced only a strangled whimper. He pushed her towards the wall, whose whitewash hung off in brittle flakes, and crackled as her cheek made contact. Her heart thundered in her chest.

'Have you been watching me, Doña Consuelo?' he said, his face appearing over her shoulder, the sourness of his winy breath in her nostrils. 'Have you been keeping a little eye out for me? Perhaps . . . since you lost your husband your bed's been a bit cold at night.'

She gasped as he slipped his hand between her bare legs. It *was* rough. An automatic reflex clamped her thighs shut. He sawed his hand up to her crotch. A voice in her head remonstrated with her for being so stupid. Her heart walloped in her throat while her brain screamed for her to say something.

'If it's money you want . . .' she said, in a voice that whispered to the flaking whitewash.

'Well,' he said, pulling his hand away, 'how much have you got? I don't come cheap, you know. Especially for the sort of thing you like.'

He took her handbag off her shoulder, flipped it open and found her wallet.

'A hundred and twenty euros!' he said, disgusted.

'Take it,' she said, her voice still stuck under her thyroid.

'Thank you, thank you very much,' he said, dropping her handbag to his feet. 'But that's not enough for what you want. Come back with the rest tomorrow.'

He pressed against her. She felt his obscene hardness against her buttocks. His face came over her shoulder once more and he kissed her on the corner of her mouth, his wine and tobacco breath and bitter little tongue slipping between her lips.

He pushed himself away, a gold ring on his finger flashed in the corner of her eye. He stepped back, kicked her handbag down the street.

'Fuck off, whore,' he said. 'You make me sick.'

The steel tips receded. Consuelo's throat still throbbed so that breathing was more like swallowing without being able to achieve either. She looked back to where he'd gone, confused at her escape. The empty cobbles shone under the yellow light. She pushed away from the wall, snatched up her handbag and ran, slipping and hobbling, down the street to the main road where she hailed a cab. She sat in the back with the city floating past her pallid face. Her hands shook too much to light the cigarette she'd managed to get into her mouth. The driver lit it for her.

At home she found money in her desk to pay for the taxi. She ran upstairs and checked the boys in their beds. She went to her own room and stripped off and looked at herself in the mirror. He hadn't marked her. She showered endlessly, soaping and resoaping herself, rinsing herself again and again.

She went back to her desk in her dressing gown and sat in the dark, feeling nauseous, head aching, waiting for dawn. When it was the earliest possible acceptable moment, she phoned Alicia Aguado and asked for an emergency appointment.

3

Juez Esteban Calderón was not on business. The urbane
and highly successful judge had told his wife, Inés, that
he was working late before going to dinner with a
group of young state judges who had come down from
Madrid on a training course. He *had* worked late and
he *had* gone to the dinner, but he'd excused himself
early and was now taking his favourite little detour
down the side of the San Marcos church to reach 'the
penthouse of promise', which overlooked the church
of Santa Isabel. He usually enjoyed smoking a cigarette
at the edge of the small, floodlit plaza, looking from
within the darkness at the fountain and the massive
portal of the church. It calmed him after long days
spent with prosecutors and policemen and kept him
out of the way of some bars around the corner, which
were frequented by colleagues. If they saw him there
it would get back to Inés and there'd be awkward questions. He also needed a few moments to rein in his
quivering sexual tension, which started every morning
when he woke up and imagined the long coppery hair
and mulatto skin of his Cuban girlfriend, Marisa

Moreno, who lived in the penthouse just visible from where he was sitting.

His cigarette hissed in a puddle where he'd tossed it, half smoked. He took off his jacket. A breeze sprayed droplets of water from the orange trees on to his back, and he caught his breath at the lash of its sudden chill. He kept to the wall of the church until he was in the darkness of the narrow street. His finger hovered over the top button of the entry phone as an accumulation of half thoughts made him hesitate: subterfuge, infidelity, fear, sex, dizziness and death. He scratched at the air above the button; these unusual thoughts made him feel that he was on the brink of something like a great change. What to do? Either step over the edge or fall back. He swallowed some thick, bitter saliva from his fast smoking. The sensuality of the lash of raindrops across his back reached that nexus of nerves in the base of his spine. The unease disappeared. His recklessness made him feel alive again and his cock leapt in his pants. He hit the buzzer.

'It's me,' he said, to the crackle of Marisa's voice.

'You sound thirsty.'

'Not thirsty,' he said, clearing his throat.

The two-man lift didn't seem to have enough air and he started panting. Its stainless steel panels reflected the absurd shape of his arousal and he rearranged himself. He brushed back his thinning hair, loosened his flamboyant tie and knocked on her door. It opened a crack and Marisa's amber eyes blinked slowly. The door fell open. She was wearing a long, orange silk shift, which nearly reached the floor. It was fastened with a single amber disc between her flat breasts. She kissed him and slipped a cube of ice from between her lips into his confused mouth and something like a firework went off in the back of his head.

She held him at bay with a single finger on his sternum. The ice cooled his tongue. She gave him an appraising look, from crown to crotch, and admonished him with a raised eyebrow. She took his jacket and hurled it into the room. He loved this whorish stuff she did, and she knew it. She dropped to her haunches, undid his belt and tugged his trousers and underpants down, then eased him profoundly into the coolness of her mouth. Calderón braced himself in the doorframe and gritted his teeth. She looked up at his agony with wide eyes. He lasted less than a minute.

She stood, turned on her heel and strode back into her apartment. Calderón pulled himself together. He didn't hear her hawking and spitting in the bathroom. He just saw her reappear from the kitchen, carrying two chilled glasses of cava.

'I thought you weren't coming,' she said, looking at the thin, gold wafer of watch on her wrist, 'and then I remembered my mother telling me that the only time a Sevillano wasn't late was for the bulls.'

Calderón was too dazed to comment. Marisa drank from her flute. Twenty gold and silver bracelets rattled on her forearm. She lit a cigarette, crossed her legs and let the shift slip away to reveal a long, slim leg, orange panties and a hard brown stomach. Calderón knew that stomach, its paper-thin skin, hard wriggling muscularity and soft coppery down. He'd laid his head on it and stroked the tight copper curls of her pubis.

'Esteban!'

He snapped out of the natural revolutions of his mind.

33

'Have you eaten?' he asked, nothing else coming to him, conversation not being one of the strengths of their relationship.

'I don't need any feeding,' she said, taking a shelled brazil nut from a bowl, and putting it between her hard, white teeth. 'I'm quite ready to be fucked.'

The nut went off in her mouth like a silenced gun and Calderón reacted like a sprinter out of the blocks. He fell into her snake-like arms and bit into her unnaturally long neck, which seemed stretched, like those of African tribal women. In fact for him, that was her attraction: part sophisticate, part savage. She'd lived in Paris, modelling for Givenchy, and travelled across the Sahara with a caravan of Tuaregs. She'd slept with a famous movie director in Los Angeles and lived with a fisherman on the beach near Maputo in Mozambique. She'd worked for an artist in New York, and spent six months in the Congo learning how to carve wood. Calderón knew all this, and believed it because Marisa was such an extraordinary creature, but he didn't have the first idea of what was going on in her head. So, like a good lawyer, he clung to these few dazzling facts.

After sex they went to bed, which for Marisa was a place to talk or sleep but not for the writhings and juices of sex. They lay naked under a sheet with light from the street in parallelograms on the wall and ceiling. The cava fizzed in glasses balanced on their chests. They shared an ashtray in the trough between their bodies.

'Shouldn't you have gone by now?' said Marisa.

'Just a little bit longer,' said Calderón, drowsy.

'What *does* Inés think you're doing all this time?' asked Marisa, for something to say.

'I'm at a dinner . . . for work.'

'You're just about the last person in the world who should be married,' she said.

'Why do you say that?'

'Well, maybe not. After all, you Sevillanos *are* very conservative. Is that why you married her?'

'Part of it.'

'What was the other part?' she asked, pointing the cone of her cigarette at his chest. 'The more interesting part.'

She burnt a hair off one of his nipples; the smell of it filled his nostrils.

'Careful,' he said, feeling the sting, 'you don't want ash all over the sheets.'

She rolled back from him, flicked her cigarette out on to the balcony.

'I like to hear the parts that people don't want to tell me about,' she said.

Her coppery hair was splayed out on the white pillow. He hadn't been able to look at her hair without thinking of the other woman he'd known with hair of the same colour. It had never occurred to him to tell anybody about the late Maddy Krugman except the police in his statement. He hadn't even talked to Inés about that night. She knew the story from the newspapers, the surface of it anyway, and that was all she'd wanted to know.

Marisa raised her head and sipped from her flute. He was attracted to her for the same reason that he'd been attracted to Maddy: the beauty, the glamour, the sexiness and the complete mystery. But what was he to her? What had he been to Maddy Krugman? That was something that occupied his spare thinking time. Especially those hours of the early morning, when he woke up next to Inés and thought that he might be dead.

'I don't really give a fuck why you married her,' said Marisa, trying a well-tested trick.

'Well, that's not what's interesting.'

'I'm not sure I need to know what *is* interesting,' said Marisa. 'Most men who think they're fascinating only ever talk about themselves . . . their successes.'

'This wasn't one of my successes,' said Calderón. 'It was one of my greatest failures.'

He'd made a snap decision to tell her. Candour was not one of his strongest suits; in his society it had a way of coming back on you, but Marisa was an outsider. He also wanted to fascinate her. Having always been the object of fascination to women he'd understood completely, he had the uncomfortable feeling of being ordinary with exotic creatures like Maddy Krugman and Marisa Moreno. Here, he thought, was an opportunity to intrigue the intriguers.

'It was about four years ago and I'd just announced my engagement to Inés,' he said. 'I was called to a situation, which looked like a murder-suicide. There were some anomalies, which meant that the detective, who, by a coincidence, happened to be the ex-husband of Inés, wanted to treat it as a double murder investigation. The victim's neighbours were American. The woman was an artist and stunningly beautiful. She was a photographer with a taste for the weird. Her name was Maddy Krugman and I fell in love with her. We had a brief but intense affair until her insane husband found out and cornered us in an apartment one night. To cut a long and painful story short, he shot her and then himself. I was lucky not to get a bullet in the head as well.'

They lay in silence. Voices came up over the balcony rail from the street. A warm breeze blew at the voile curtains, which billowed into the room, bringing the smell of rain and the promise of hot weather in the morning.

'And that's why you married Inés.'

'Maddy was dead. I was very badly shaken. Inés represented stability.'

'Did you tell her you'd fallen in love with this woman?'

'We never talked about it.'

'And what now . . . four years later?'

'I feel nothing for Inés,' said Calderón, which was not quite the whole truth. He did feel something for her. He hated her. He could hardly bear to share her bed, had to steel himself to her touch, and he couldn't understand why. He had no idea where it came from. She hadn't changed. She had been both good to him and for him after the Maddy incident. This feeling of dying he had when he was with her in bed was a symptom. Of what, he could not say.

'Well, Esteban, you're a member of a very large club.'

'Have you ever been married?'

'You *are* joking,' said Marisa. 'I watched the soap opera of my parents' marriage for fifteen years. That was enough to warn me off that particular bourgeois institution.'

'And what are you doing with me?' asked Calderón, fishing for something, but not sure what. 'It doesn't get more bourgeois than having an affair with a state judge.'

'Being bourgeois is a state of mind,' she said. 'What you do means nothing to me. It has no bearing on us. We're having an affair and it will carry on until it burns out. But I'm not going to get married and you already are.'

'You said I was the last person in the world who should be married,' said Calderón.

'People get married if they want to have kids and fit into society, or, if they're suckers, they marry their dream.'

'I didn't marry *my* dream,' said Calderón. 'I married everybody else's dream. I was the brilliant young judge, Inés was the brilliant and beautiful young prosecutor. We were the "golden couple", as seen on TV.'

'You don't have any children,' said Marisa. 'Get divorced.'

'It's not so easy.'

'Why not? It's taken you four years to find out that you're incompatible,' said Marisa. 'Get out now while you're still young.'

'You've had a lot of lovers.'

'I might have been to bed with a lot of men but I've only had four lovers.'

'And how do you define a lover?' asked Calderón, still fishing.

'Someone I love and who loves me.'

'Sounds simple.'

'It can be . . . as long as you don't let life fuck it up.'

The question burned inside Calderón. Did she love him? But almost as soon as it came into his mind he had to ask himself whether he loved her. They cancelled each other out. He'd been fucking her for nine months. That wasn't quite fair, or was it? Marisa could hear his brain working. She recognized the sound. Men always assumed their brains were silent rather than grinding away like sabotaged machinery.

38

'So now you're going to tell me,' said Marisa, 'that you can't get a divorce for all those bourgeois reasons – career, status, social acceptance, property and money.'

That *was* it, thought Calderón, his face going slack in the dark. That was *precisely* why he couldn't get a divorce. He would lose everything. He had only just scraped his career back together again after the Maddy debacle. Being related to the Magistrado Juez Decano de Sevilla had helped, but so had his marriage to Inés. If he divorced her now his career might easily drift, his friends would slip away, he would lose his apartment and he would be poorer. Inés would make sure of all that.

'There is, of course, a bourgeois solution to that,' said Marisa.

'What?' said Calderón, turning to look at her between her upturned nipples, suddenly hopeful.

'You could murder her,' she said, throwing open her hands, easy peasy.

Calderón smiled at first, not quite registering what she had said. His smile turned into a grin and then he laughed. As he laughed his head bounced on Marisa's taut stomach and it bounced higher and higher as her muscles tightened with laughter. He sat up spluttering at the brilliant absurdity of her idea.

'Me, the leading Juez de Instrucción in Seville, killing his wife?'

'Ask her ex-husband for some advice,' said Marisa, her stomach still contracting with laughter. 'He should know how to commit the perfect murder.'

4

Manuela Falcón was in bed, but not sleeping. It was 5.30 in the morning. She had the bedside light on, knees up, flicking through *Vogue* but not reading, not even looking at the pictures. She had too much on her mind: her property portfolio, the money she owed to the banks, the mortgage repayments, the lack of rental income, the lawyer's fees, the two deeds due to be signed this morning, which would release her capital into beautifully fluid funds of cash.

'For God's sake, relax,' said Angel, waking up in bed next to her, still groggy with sleep and nursing a small cognac-induced hangover. 'What are you so anxious about?'

'I can't believe you've asked that question,' said Manuela. 'The deeds, *this* morning?'

Angel Zarrías blinked into his pillow. He'd forgotten.

'Look, my darling,' he said, rolling over, 'you know that nothing happens, even if you think about it *all* the time. It only happens . . .'

'Yes, I know, Angel, it only happens when it happens.

40

But even you can understand that there's uncertainty *before* it happens.'

'But if you don't sleep and you churn it over in your head in an endless washing cycle it has no effect on the outcome, so you might as well forget about it. Handle the horror if it happens, but don't torture yourself with the theory of it.'

Manuela flicked through the pages of *Vogue* even more viciously, but she felt better. Angel could do that to her. He was older. He had authority. He had experience.

'It's all right for you,' she said, gently, 'you don't owe six hundred thousand euros to the bank.'

'But I also don't own nearly two million euros' worth of property.'

'I own one million eight hundred thousand euros' worth of property. I owe six hundred thousand to the bank. The lawyer's fees are . . . Forget it. Let's not talk about numbers. They make me sick. Nothing has any value until it's sold.'

'Which is what you're about to do,' said Angel, in his most solid, reinforced concrete voice.

'Anything can happen,' she said, turning a page so viciously she tore it.

'But it tends not to.'

'The market's nervous.'

'Which is why you're selling. Nobody's going to withdraw in the next eight hours,' he said, struggling to sit up in bed. 'Most people would kill to be in your position.'

'With two empty properties, no rent and four thousand a month going out?'

'Well, clearly I'm looking at it from a more advantageous perspective.'

41

Manuela liked this. However hard she tried, she couldn't get Angel to participate in her catalogue of imagined horrors. His objective authority made her feel quite girlish. She hadn't yet got to the point of recognizing what their relationship had become, how it fitted with her powerful needs. All she knew was that Angel was a colossal comfort to her.

'Relax,' said Angel, pulling her to him, kissing the top of her head.

'Wouldn't it be great to be able to compress time and just *be* in tomorrow evening now,' she said, snuggling up to him, 'with money in the bank and the summer free?'

'Let's have a celebratory dinner at Salvador Rojo tonight.'

'I was thinking that myself,' she said, 'but I was too superstitious to book it. We could ask Javier. He could bring Laura so you can have someone to flirt with.'

'How very considerate of you,' he said, kissing her head again.

When Angel and Manuela had met it seemed that the only thing holding her life together was her legal battle over Javier's right to have inherited the house in which he was living. They'd met in her lawyer's office, where Angel was sorting out his late wife's estate. As soon as they'd shaken hands she'd felt something cave in high up around her stomach and no man had ever done that to her before. They left the lawyer's office and went for a drink and, having never looked at older men, having always gone for 'boys', she immediately saw the point. Older men looked after you. You didn't have to look after them.

The more she found out about Angel the more she

fell for him. He was a phenomenally charming man, a committed politician (sometimes a little *too* committed), right wing, conservative, a Catholic, a lover of the bulls, and from an established family. In politics he'd been able to broker agreements between fanatically opposed factions just because neither party wanted to be disliked by him. He'd been 'someone' in the Partido Popular in Andalucía but had quit in a fury over the impossibility of getting anything to change. Recently he'd joined forces, in a public relations capacity, with a smaller right-wing party called Fuerza Andalucía, which was run by his old friend, Eduardo Rivero. He contributed a political column for the *ABC* newspaper and was also their highly respected bullfight commentator. With all these talents at his disposal it hadn't taken him long to bring Javier and Manuela back together again.

'All energy expended on court cases like yours is negative energy,' Angel had told her. 'That negative energy dominates your life, so that the rest of it has to go on hold. The only way to restart your life is to bring positive energy back into it.'

'And how do I do that?' she'd asked, looking at this huge source of positive energy in front of her with her big brown eyes.

'Court cases use up resources, not just financial ones, but physical and emotional ones, too. So you have to be productive,' he said. 'What do you want from your life at the moment?'

'That house!' she'd said, despite being pretty keen on Angel right then, too.

'It's yours, Javier has offered it to you.'

'There's the small matter of one million euros . . .'

'But he hasn't said you can't have it,' said Angel.

43

'And it's much more productive to make money in order to buy something you really want, than to throw it away on useless lawyers.'

'He's not useless,' she said, and ran out of steam.

There were a few thousand other reasons she had stacked up against Angel's stunningly simple logic, but the source of most of them was her miserable emotional state, which was not something she wanted to peel back for him to see. So, she agreed with him, sold her veterinary practice at the beginning of 2003, borrowed money against the property she had inherited in El Puerto de Santa Maria and invested it in Seville's booming property market. After three years of buying, renovating and selling she had forgotten about Javier's house, the court case and that hollow feeling at the top of her stomach. She now lived with Angel in a penthouse apartment overlooking the majestic, tree-lined Plaza Cristo de Burgos in the middle of the old city and her life was full and about to be even sweeter.

'How did it go last night?' asked Manuela. 'I can tell you wound up on the brandy.'

'Gah!' said Angel, wincing at some gripe in his intestines.

'No smoking for you until after coffee this morning.'

'Maybe my breath could become a cheap form of renewable energy,' said Angel, fingering some sleep out of his eye. 'In fact everyone's breath could, because all we do is spout hot, alcoholic air.'

'Is the master of positive energy getting a little bit bored with his cronies?'

'Not bored. They're my friends,' said Angel, shrugging. 'It's one of the advantages of age that we can tell each other the same stories over and over and still laugh.'

'Age is a state of mind, and you're still young,' said Manuela. 'Maybe you should go back to the commercial side of your public relations business. Forget politics and all those self-important fools.'

'And finally she reveals what she thinks of my closest friends.'

'I like your friends, it's just . . . the politics,' said Manuela. 'Endless talk but nothing ever happens.'

'Maybe you're right,' said Angel, nodding. 'The last time there was an event in this country was the horror of 11th March 2004, and look what happened: the whole country pulled together and by due process of democracy kicked out a perfectly good government. Then we bowed down to the terrorists and pulled out of Iraq. And after that? We sank back into the comfort of our lives.'

'And drank too much brandy.'

'Exactly,' said Angel, looking at her with his hair exploded in all directions. 'You know what someone was saying last night?'

'Was this the interesting bit?' she said, teasing him on.

'We need a return to benevolent dictatorship,' said Angel, throwing up his hands in mock exasperation.

'You might find yourselves out on a limb there,' said Manuela. 'People don't like turmoil with troops and tanks on the streets. They want a cold beer, a tapa and something stupid to watch on TV.'

'My point entirely,' said Angel, slapping his stomach. 'Nobody listened. We've got a population dying of decadence, so morally moribund that they no longer know what they want, apart from knee-jerk consumption, and my "cronies" think that they'll be *loved* if they do these people the favour of mounting a coup.'

'I don't want to see you on television, standing on a desk in Parliament with a gun in your hand.'

'I'll have to lose some weight first,' said Angel.

Calderón came to with a jolt and a sense of real panic left over from a dream he could not recollect. He was surprised to see Marisa's long brown back in the bed beside him, instead of Inés's white nightdress. He'd overslept. It was now 6 a.m. and he would have to go back to his apartment and deal with some very awkward questions from Inés.

His frantic leap from the bed woke Marisa. He dressed, shaking his head at the slug trails of dried semen on his thigh.

'Take a shower,' said Marisa.

'No time.'

'Anyway, she's not an idiot – *so* you tell me.'

'No, she's not,' said Calderón, looking for his other shoe, 'but as long as certain rules are obeyed then the whole thing can be glossed over.'

'This must be the bourgeois protocol for affairs outside marriage.'

'That's right,' said Calderón, irritated by her. 'You can't stay out all night because that is making a complete joke out of the institution.'

'What's the cut-off point between a "serious" marriage and a "joke" one?' asked Marisa. 'Three o'clock . . . three thirty? No. That's OK. I think by four o'clock it's ridiculous. By four thirty it is a complete joke. By six, six thirty . . . it's a farce.'

'By six it's a tragedy,' said Calderón, searching the floor madly. 'Where is my *fucking* shoe?'

'Under the chair,' said Marisa. 'And don't forget your camera on the coffee table. I've left a present or two on it for you.'

He threw on his jacket, pocketed the camera, dug his foot into his shoe.

'How did you find my camera?' he asked, kneeling down by the bed.

'I went through your jacket while you were asleep,' she said. 'I come from a bourgeois family; I kick against it, but I know all the tricks. Don't worry, I didn't erase all those stupid shots of your lawyers' dinner to prove to your very intelligent wife that you weren't out all night fucking your girlfriend.'

'Well, thanks very much for that.'

'And I haven't been naughty.'

'No?'

'I told you I left some presents on the camera for you. Just don't let her see.'

He nodded, suddenly in a hurry again. They kissed. Going down in the lift he tidied himself up, got everything tucked away and rubbed his face into life to prepare for the lie which he practised. Even he saw the two micro movements of his eyebrows, which Javier Falcón had told him was the first and surest sign of a liar. If he knew that, then Inés would know it, too.

No taxis out at this early hour of the morning. He should have called for one. He set off at a fast walk. Memories ricocheted around his mind, which seemed to dip in and out of his consciousness. The lie. The truth. The reality. The dream. And it came back to him with the same sense of panic he'd had on waking in

Marisa's apartment: his hands closing around Inés's slim throat. He was throttling her, but she wasn't turning puce or purple and her tongue wasn't thickening with blood and protruding. She was looking up at him with her eyes full of love. And, yes, she was stroking his forearms, encouraging him to do it. The bourgeois solution to awkward divorces – murder. Absurd. He knew from his work with the homicide squad that the first person to be grilled in a murder case was the spouse.

The streets were still wet from last night's rain, the cobbles greasy. He was sweating and the smell of Marisa came up off his shirt. It occurred to him that he'd never felt guilty. He didn't know what it was other than a legal state. Since he'd been married to Inés he'd had affairs with four women of whom Marisa had lasted the longest. He'd also had one-night stands or afternoons with two other women. And there was the prostitute in Barcelona, but he didn't like to think of that. He'd even had sex with one of these women whilst having an affair with another as a married man, which must make him a serial philanderer. Except it didn't feel like philandering. There was supposed to be something enjoyable about philandering. It was romantic, wasn't it . . . in the eighteenth-century sense of the word? But what he'd been doing was not enjoyable. He was trying to fill a hole, which, with every affair, grew bigger. So what was this expanding void? Now that would be a thing to answer, if he could ever find the time to think about it.

He slipped on a cobble, half fell, scuffed his hand on the pavement. It pulled him out of his head and on to more practical business. He'd have to have a shower as soon as he got in. Marisa was in his sinuses.

Maybe he should have had a shower before he left, but then there would have been the smell of Marisa's soap. Then another revelation. What did he care? Why the grand pretence? Inés knew. They'd had fights – never about his affairs, but about ridiculous stuff, which was a cover for the unmentionable. She could have got out. She could have left him years ago, but she'd stayed. That was significant.

The graze on his hand was stinging. His thoughts made him feel stronger. He wasn't afraid of Inés. She could strike fear into others. He'd seen her in court. But not him. He had the upper hand. He fucked around and she stayed.

His apartment block on Calle San Vicente appeared before him. He opened the door with a flourish. He didn't know whether it was the conclusion he'd arrived at, his stinging hand or the fact that he tripped up on the stairs because the decorators, those idle sods, had pushed their dustsheets to one side rather than clearing them away – but he began to feel just a little bit cruel.

The first-floor apartment was silent. It was 6.30 a.m. He went to his study and emptied the pockets of his suit on to his desk in the dark. He took off his jacket and trousers and left them on a chair and went to the bathroom. Inés was asleep. He stripped off his pants and socks, threw them in the laundry basket and showered.

Inés was *not* asleep. She lay with her shiny, dark eyes blinking in the sepia light as morning crept through the louvred shutters. She had been awake since 4.30 a.m. when she'd found her husband's side of the bed vacant. She'd sat up in bed, arms folded across her flat chest, her brain seething. She'd run the marathon of her thoughts for two hours, her insides molten with rage at the humiliation of finding his undented pillow. But then she would suddenly feel weak at the thought of facing this latest demonstration of his infidelity, because that's what it was – a demonstration.

In those hours she realized that the only area of her life that was functioning was her work, which now bored her. Not that the work had changed in any way, but her perspective had. She wanted to be a wife and mother. She wanted to live in a big old house with a patio, inside the city walls. She wanted to go for walks in the park, meet her friends for lunch, take her children to see her parents.

None of that had happened. After the American bitch had been removed from the scene, she and Esteban had come together, had, in her mind, grown closer. She had stopped using contraceptives without telling him, wanting to surprise him, but her periods kept coming with plodding regularity. She'd gone for a check-up and been pronounced a perfectly healthy female of the species. After sex one morning she'd saved a sample of his sperm and taken it for a fertility test. The result was that he was a man of exceptional virility. Had he known, he would have framed the result and hung it next to their wedding photograph.

The sale of her apartment had gone through quickly. She'd banked the money and started looking for her dream home. But Esteban loathed the houses that she wanted to buy and refused to look at them. The property market boomed. The money she'd got for her apartment now looked paltry. Her dream became an impossibility. They lived in his very masculine, aggressively modern apartment on the Calle San Vicente and he became angry if she tried to change a single detail. He wouldn't even let her put a chain on the door, but that was because he didn't want to have to be let in by her reeking of sex after a night out.

Their sex life began to falter. She knew he was having affairs from the tireless grind of his lovemaking and the paucity of his ejaculations. She tried to be more daring. He made her feel foolish, as if her proposed 'games' were ridiculous. Then suddenly he'd taken up her offer to 'play games' but given her debasing roles, seemingly inspired by internet porn. She subjected herself to his ministrations, hiding her pain and shame in the pillow.

At least she wasn't fat. She inspected herself minutely in the mirror every day. It satisfied her to see the deflation of her bust, her individual ribs and her concave thighs. Sometimes she would feel dizzy in court. Her friends told her she'd never get pregnant. She smiled at them, her pale skin stretched tight over her beautiful face, her aura frighteningly beatific.

Inés was toying with the idea of a massive confrontation when she heard Esteban put his key in the lock. Her stick-thin forearms seemed to have grown more hair and they made her feel curiously weak. She sank down into the bed and pretended to be asleep.

She heard him empty his pockets and go to the bathroom. The shower came on. She ran barefoot to his study, saw his suit and sniffed it over like a dog: cigarettes, perfume, old sex. Her eyes were riveted to the digital camera. She touched it with her knuckle. Still warm. She burned to know what was on its memory. The shower door rolled open. She ran back to bed and lay with her heart beating fast as a cat's.

His weight tipped her feather-light frame in the bed. She waited for his breathing to settle into the pattern that she knew was his sleep. Her heart slowed. Her mind cooled. She slid out of the bed. He didn't move. In the study she pressed the camera's quick-view button and caught her breath as a miniature Marisa appeared on the screen. She was naked on the sofa, legs apart, hands covering her pubis. Inés pressed again. Marisa naked, kneeling and looking backwards over her shoulder. The whore. She pressed again and again and only found her husband's alibi of the judges' dinner. She went back to the whore. Who was she? The black bitch. She had to know.

Inés's laptop was in the hall. She took it into the kitchen and booted it up. In the grey-bar time she went back to his study and scoured the shelves for the download lead. Back to the kitchen. Opened up the camera, plugged in the lead, connected it to her laptop. Total concentration.

The icon appeared on the screen. The software automatically loaded. She clicked on 'import' and clenched her fist as she saw she was going to have to download fifty-four shots to get the ones she wanted. She stared at the screen, willing it to process faster. She heard only the breathing of the computer's fan and the flickering of the hard disk. She didn't hear the bedclothes stir. She didn't hear his bare foot on the wooden floor. She didn't even hear his question properly.

His voice did turn her round. She was conscious of her cotton nightdress on the points of her shoulders, its hem brushing the tops of her thighs, as she took in the full-frontal nudity of her husband standing in the frame of the kitchen door.

'What's going on?' he asked.

'What?' said Inés, her eyes unable to look anywhere other than his treacherous genitals.

He repeated his question.

The adrenaline spike was so powerful she wasn't sure that her heart could cope with the sudden surge.

After nearly twenty years' experience in the criminal element Calderón could recognize terror when he saw it. The wide eyes, the mouth neither open nor closed, the paralysed facial muscles.

'What's going on?' he asked, for a third time but with no sleep in his voice, pure weight.

'Nothing,' she said, keeping her back to the laptop, but unable to stop the reflex action of her arms fanning out to prevent him from seeing her laptop.

Calderón swept her aside, not roughly, but she was so light she had to stop her fragile ribs from cracking against the edge of the black granite work surface. He saw his camera, the lead, the thumbnails of the lawyers' dinner appearing in the photo library. And then plink, plink. Two shots of Marisa: *My present to you*. It was embarrassing, incriminating and worse: it was the little boy being found out.

'Who is she?' asked Inés, her finger ends white against the black granite.

His look was murderous and in no way offset by the ridiculousness of his nudity.

'Who is she, that you can stay out all night, leaving your wife alone in the marital bed?'

The words incensed him, which was Inés's calculation. Her fear had vanished. She wanted something from him – his concentrated attention.

'Who is she, that you can whore with her until six in the morning, in defiance of your marital vows?'

Another calculated sentence, using some of the oratory she employed in court.

He turned on her, with the slow intent of an animal who's found a rival on his territory. The thickness around his belly, the shrivelled penis, the slim thighs should have made him laughable, but his head was dipped down and his eyes looked up from under his brow. His rage was palpable. Still Inés couldn't help herself. The taunts leapt from her lips.

'Do you fuck her like you fuck me? Do you make her shout with pain?'

Inés did not finish because she was unaccountably on the floor, with her feet pedalling against the white marble tiles, trying to fight air back into her lungs. She focused on his toes, the knuckles crimped as they gripped. He kicked her. His big toe invaded her kidney. She bit on air. She was shocked. It was the first time he'd ever hit her. She'd provoked him. She'd wanted a reaction. But she had been shocked by his restraint. She'd thought he would lash out, backhand her across the face to shut that taunting uxorial mouth, fatten her lip, bruise her cheek. She wanted to wear the badge of his violence to show the world what he was really like and draw some daily remorse from him until the damage faded. But he'd hit her under the arch of her ribs, kicked her in the side.

Her chest creaked as she found the motor memory to breathe again. She felt her husband's hand at the back of her head, stroking. You see, he did love her. Now for the remorse and the tenderness. This was just another fling . . . But he wasn't stroking her, he was

54

reaching into her hair, he was sheafing it. His nails dug into her scalp. He shook her head as if she were a dog, caught by the scruff, and stood up from his crouch. She hadn't found her feet and she hung from his hand. He dragged her from the kitchen, hauled her down the corridor and flung her at the bed. She bounced and rolled off to the side. Three strides and he was on her again. She scrambled under the bed.

It hadn't worked out as she'd thought. His hand reached for her under the bed, grabbing at her night-dress. She flinched away from it. His face appeared, hideous with rage. He stood up. His feet moved off. She watched them, as if they were loaded weapons. They left the room. He swore and slammed the door. Her scalp burned. Her fear was overriding all other emotions. She couldn't scream, she couldn't cry.

Under the bed was good. There were childhood memories of safety, of observing in secrecy, but they couldn't contain her confusion. Her brain lunged at what she wanted to be certainties, but they wouldn't support her. Instead she found herself trying to accommodate his behaviour. She had proved his infidelity to him. She had humiliated him. He was angry because he felt guilty. That was natural. You lashed out at the one you loved. That was it, wasn't it? He didn't want to be whoring with that black bitch. He just couldn't help himself. He was an alpha male, a virile, high-octane performer. She shouldn't be so hard on him. She held on to her side and squeezed her eyes shut at a jab of pain in her kidney.

The door swung open, the feet came back into the room. His presence made her shrink. He took fresh socks and pants from the drawer and put them on. He stepped into a pair of trousers and took a crisp, white shirt, ironed by the laundry where he still sent his clothes. He shook it out and drove his arms into the sleeves, shot the cuffs. He whipped a crimson tie into a perfect knot. He was efficient, vigorous and precise. He rammed those brutal feet into a pair of shoes, threw on a jacket – his savagery now perfectly disguised.

'I'm working late tonight,' he said, his tone back to normal.

The apartment door clicked shut. Inés crawled out from under the bed and flopped against the wall. She sat with her legs splayed out, her hands helpless by her sides. The first sob jolted her away from the wall.

5

Falcón came to in the profound darkness of his shuttered bedroom. He lay there in his private universe,
contemplating last night's events. After the disappointment at Consuelo's restaurant the drink with
Laura had gone better than expected. They'd agreed to
see each other as friends. She was only a little offended
that he was ending their affair with, as he'd told her,
no other prospect in sight.

He showered and put on a dark suit and white shirt
and folded a tie into his pocket. He had meetings
planned all morning after he'd been to see the Médico
Forense. It was a morning of shimmering brilliance,
with not a cloud in the sky. The rain had cleansed the
atmosphere of all that puzzling electricity.

A temperature gauge outside in the street told him
it was 16°C while the radio warned that a great heat
was about to descend on Seville and by evening they
should expect temperatures in excess of 36°C.

The Forensic Institute was next to the Hospital de
la Macarena behind the Andalucían Parliament, which
itself looked across the road to the Basilica de la

Macarena, just inside the old city walls. At 8.15 a.m. Falcón was early, but the Médico Forense had already arrived.

Dr Pintado had the file open on his desk and was reminding himself of the detail of the autopsy. They shook hands, sat down and he resumed his reading.

'What I concentrated on in this case,' he said, still scanning the pages, 'apart from the cause of death, which was straightforward – he was poisoned with potassium cyanide – was giving you as much help as possible on the identification of the body.'

'Potassium cyanide?' said Falcón. 'That's not exactly in keeping with the ruthlessness of the post-mortem operations. Was it injected?'

'No, ingested,' said Pintado, other things on his mind. 'The face . . . I might be able to help you with that, or rather I have a friend who is interested in helping. You remember I was telling you about a case I handled in Bilbao, where they made a facial model from a skull found in a shallow grave?'

'It cost a fortune.'

'That's right, and you don't get resources like that for any old murder.'

'So how much does your friend cost?'

'He's free.'

'And who is he?'

'He's a sort of sculptor, but he's not that interested in the body, just faces.'

'Would I have heard of him?'

'No. He's strictly amateur. His name is Miguel Covo. He's seventy-four years old and retired,' said Pintado. 'But he's been working with faces for nearly sixty years. He builds them out of clay, makes moulds for wax, and carves them out of stone, although that's quite a recent development.'

'What's he proposing and why is it free?'

'Well, he's never done this kind of thing before, but he wants to try,' said Pintado. 'I let him take a plaster cast of the head last night.'

'OK, so there's no decision,' said Falcón.

'He'll make up a half-dozen models, do some sketches and then start working up the face. He'll paint it, too, and give it hair – real hair. His studio can give you the creeps, especially if he likes you and introduces you to his mother.'

'I've always got on well with mothers.'

'He keeps her in a cupboard,' said Dr Pintado. 'Just a model of her, I mean.'

'It would be cruel to keep a woman in her nineties in a cupboard.'

'She died when he was small, which was when his fascination with faces started. He wanted the photographs of her to be more real. So he recreated her. It was the only time he fashioned a body. She's in that cupboard with real hair, make-up, her own clothes and shoes.'

'So, he's weird, too?'

'Of course he is,' said Pintado, 'but likeably weird. You might not want to invite him to dinner with the Comisario and his wife, though.'

'Why not?' said Falcón. 'It would make a change from the opera.'

'Anyway, he'll call you when he has something, but . . . not tomorrow.'

'What else have you got?'

'It's all helpful, but not as helpful as a physical image,'

said Pintado. 'I worked with a guy who did forensics on mass graves in Bosnia and I learnt a bit from him. The first thing is dental. I've made a full set of digital X-rays and notes about each tooth. He's had extensive orthodontic work done to get the teeth all straight and looking perfect.'

'How old is this guy?'

'Mid forties.'

'And normally you'd have that sort of work done in your early teens.'

'Exactly.'

'And there wasn't a lot of orthodontic work being done in Spain in the mid seventies.'

'Most likely it was done in America,' said Pintado. 'Apart from that, there's nothing much else to go on, dentally. He's had no major work done, and only a molar missing on the lower right side.'

'Have you found any distinguishing marks on the outside of the body – moles, birthmarks?'

'No, but I did come across something interesting on his hands.'

'Forgive me, Doctor, but . . .'

'I know. They were severed. But I checked the lymph nodes to see what was deposited there,' said Pintado. 'I'm sure our friend had a small tattoo on each hand.'

'I don't suppose there's a snapshot of it in the lymph node?' asked Falcón.

'Lymph nodes are quite clever about killing bacteria and neutralizing toxins, but their talent for recreating images from tattoo ink, introduced into the bloodstream via the hand, is extremely limited. There was a trace of ink and that was all.'

'What about surgery?'

'There's good news and bad there,' said Pintado. 'He's had surgery, but it was a hernia operation, which is just about the world's most common procedure. His was also the most common type of inguinal hernia, so he has a scar on the right side of his pubis. I'd guess it was about three years old, but I'll get one of the vascular surgeons to come over and confirm that for me. Then we'll take a look at the mesh they used to patch the hernia and hopefully he'll be able to tell me who supplied it, then you can find the hospitals *they* supply . . . and, I know, it's going to take a lot of work and time.'

'Maybe he had that done in America as well,' said Falcón.

'Like I said: good news and bad.'

'What about his hair?' asked Falcón. 'They scalped him.'

'He had hair that was at least long enough to cover his collar.'

'How do you get that?'

'He's been on the beach this year,' said Pintado, turning some photographs around for Falcón to look at. 'You can see the tan lines on his arms and legs, but if you turn him over you don't see any tan line at the back of his neck. In fact, if you look, it's quite white compared to the rest of his back, which to me means that it rarely sees the sun.'

'Would you describe him as "white"?' asked Falcón. 'His skin colour didn't look Northern European to me.'

'No. He's olive-skinned.'

'Do you think he was Spanish?'

'Without doing any genetic testing, I would say that he was Mediterranean.'

'Any scars?'

'Nothing significant,' said Pintado. 'He'd sustained a fracture to his skull, but it's years old.'

'Anything interesting about the structure of his body that would give us an idea of what he did?'

'Well, he wasn't a bodybuilder,' said Pintado. 'Spine, shoulder and elbows indicate a deskbound, sedentary life. I'd say that his feet didn't spend much time in shoes. The heels are more splayed than usual, with a lot of hardened skin.'

'As you said, he liked the sun,' said Falcón.

'He also smoked cannabis and I would say he was a regular user, which could be thought of as unusual in someone in his mid forties,' said Pintado. 'Kids smoke dope, but if you're still doing it in your forties it's because it's your milieu . . . you're an artist, or a musician, or hanging out with that sort of crowd.'

'So he's a desk worker with long hair, who spent time in the sun, not wearing shoes, and smoking dope.'

'A hard-working hippy.'

'They might have been like that in the seventies, but it's not the profile of a modern-day drug smuggler,' said Falcón. 'And potassium cyanide would be an unusual method of execution for people with 9mm handguns in their waistbands.'

The two men sat back from the desk. Falcón flicked through the photographs from the file hoping that something else might jump out at him. He was already thinking about the university and the Bellas Artes, but he didn't want to confine himself at this early stage.

In this momentary silence the two men looked up at each other, as if they were on the brink of the same idea. From beyond the grey walls of the Facultad de

Medicina came the unmistakable boom of a significant explosion, not far away.

Gloria Alanis was ready for work. By this time she would normally be on her way to her first client meeting, thinking how much, as it receded in the rear-view mirror, she hated the drab seventies apartment block where she lived in the barrio of El Cerezo. She was a sales rep for a stationery company but her area of operation was Huelva. On the first Tuesday of every month there was a meeting of the sales team at the head office in Seville, followed by a team-building exercise, a lunch and then a mini-conference to show and discuss new products and promotions.

It meant that for one day during the month, she could put breakfast on the table for her husband and two children. She could also take her eight-year-old daughter, Lourdes, to school, while her husband delivered their three-year-old son, Pedro, to the pre-school which was visible from the back window of their fifth-floor apartment.

On this morning, instead of hating her apartment, she was looking down on the heads of her children and husband and feeling an unusual sensation of warmth and affection early in the week. Her husband sensed this, grabbed her and pulled her on to his lap.

'Fernando,' she said, warning him, in case he tried anything too salacious in front of the children.

'I was thinking,' he whispered in her ear, his lips tickling her lobe.

'It's always dangerous when you start doing that,' she said, smiling at the children, who were now interested.

'I was thinking there should be more of us,' he whispered. 'Gloria, Fernando, Lourdes, Pedro and . . .'

'You're crazy,' she said, loving those lips on her ear, saying these things.

'We always talked about having four, didn't we?'

'But that was before we knew how much two cost,' she said. 'Now we work all day and still don't have enough money to get out of this apartment or take a holiday.'

'I have a secret,' he said.

She knew he didn't.

'If it's a lottery ticket, I don't want to see it.'

'It's not a lottery ticket.'

She knew what it was: wild hope.

'My God,' he said, suddenly looking at his watch. 'Hey, Pedro, we've got to get going, man.'

'Tell us the secret,' said the children.

He lifted Gloria up and put her on her feet.

'If I tell you that, it's not a secret any more,' he said. 'You have to wait for the secret to be revealed.'

'Tell us now!'

'This evening,' he said, kissing Lourdes on the head and taking Pedro's tiny hand.

Gloria went to the door with them. She kissed Pedro, who was staring at his feet, and not much interested. She kissed her husband on the mouth and whispered on his lips:

'I hate you.'

'By this evening you'll love me again.'

She went back to the breakfast table and sat opposite Lourdes. There were another fifteen minutes before they had to leave. They spent a few minutes looking at one of Lourdes' drawings before going to the window.

Fernando and Pedro appeared below in the car park in front of the pre-school. They waved. Fernando held Pedro above his head and he waved back.

Having delivered the boy to school, Fernando walked off between the apartment blocks to the main road to catch the bus to work. Gloria turned back into the room. Lourdes was already at the table working on another drawing. Gloria sipped her coffee and played with her daughter's silky hair. Fernando and his secrets. He played these games to keep them amused and their hopes up that they would eventually be able to buy their own apartment, but the property prices had exploded and they now knew that they would be renting for the rest of their lives. Gloria was never going to be anything other than a rep and, though Fernando kept saying he was going to take a plumbing course, he still needed to make the money he did as a labourer on the construction site. They'd been lucky to find this apartment with such a cheap rent. They were lucky to have two healthy children. As Fernando said: 'We might not be rich, but we *are* lucky and luck will serve us better than all the money in the world.'

She didn't immediately associate the shuddering tremor beneath her feet with the booming crash that came from the outside world. It was a noise so loud that her rib cage seemed to clutch at her spine and drive the air out of her lungs. The coffee cup jumped out of her hand and broke on the floor.

'MAMÁ!' screamed Lourdes, but there was nothing for Gloria to hear, she saw only her daughter's wide-eyed horror and grabbed her.

Terrible things happened simultaneously. Windows shattered. Cracks and giant fissures opened up in the walls. Daylight appeared where it shouldn't. Level horizons tilted. Doorframes folded. Solid concrete flexed. The ceiling crowded the floor. Walls broke in half. Water spurted from nowhere. Electricity crackled and sparked under broken tiles. A wardrobe shot out of sight. Gravity showed them its remorselessness. Mother and daughter were falling. Their small, fragile bodies were hurtling downwards in a miasma of bricks, steel, concrete, wire, tubing, furniture and dust. There was no time for words. There was no sound, because the sound was already so loud it rendered everything else silent. There wasn't even any fear, because it had all become grossly incomprehensible. There was just the sickening plummet, the stunning impact and then a vast blackness, as of a great receding universe.

'What the fuck was that?' said Pintado.

Falcón knew exactly what it was. He'd heard an ETA car bomb explode when he was working in Barcelona. This sounded big. He kicked back his chair and ran out of the Institute without replying to Pintado's question. He punched the Jefatura's number into his mobile as he left. His first thought was that it was something in the Santa Justa station, the high-speed AVE arriving from Madrid. The railway station was less than a kilometre away to the southeast of the hospital.

'*Diga*,' said Ramírez.

'There's been a bomb, José Luis . . .'

'I heard it even out here,' said Ramírez.

'I'm at the Institute. It sounded close. Get me some news.'

'Hold it.'

Falcón ran past the receptionist, the mobile pressed

to his ear, listening to Ramírez's feet pounding down the corridor and up the stairs and people shouting in the Jefatura. The traffic had stopped everywhere. Drivers and passengers were getting out of their cars, looking to the northeast at a plume of black smoke.

'The reports we're getting,' said Ramírez, panting, 'is that there's been an explosion in an apartment block on the corner of Calle Blanca Paloma and Calle Los Romeros in the barrio of El Cerezo.'

'Where's that? I don't know it. It must be close because I can see the smoke.'

Ramírez found a wall map and gave rapid instructions.

'Is there any report of a gas leak?' asked Falcón, knowing this was wildly optimistic, like the so-called power surge on the day of the London underground bombings.

'I'm checking the gas company.'

Falcón sprinted through the hospital. People were running, but there was no panic, no shouting. They had been training for this moment. Everyone in a white coat was making for the casualty department. Orderlies were sprinting with empty trolleys. Nurses ran with boxes of saline. Plasma was on the move. Falcón slammed through endless double doors until he hit the main street and the wall of sound: a cacophony of sirens as ambulances swung out into the street.

The main road was miraculously clear of traffic. As he crossed the empty lanes he saw cars pulling up on to pavements. There were no police. This was the work of ordinary citizens, who knew that this stretch of road had to be kept clear to ferry the wounded. Ambulances careered down the street two abreast, whooping and delirious, with lights flashing queasily, in air that was filling with a grey/pink dust and smoke that billowed out from behind the apartment blocks.

At the crossroads bloodstained people stumbled about on their own or were being carried, or walked towards the hospital with handkerchiefs, tissues and kitchen roll held to foreheads, ears and cheeks. These were the superficially wounded victims, the ones sliced by flying glass and metal, the ones some distance from the epicentre, who would never make it into the top flight of disaster statistics but who might lose the sight in an eye, or their hearing from perforated eardrums, bear facial scars for the rest of their lives, lose the use of a finger or a hand, never walk again without a limp. They were being helped by the lucky ones, those who didn't even have a scratch as the air whistled with flying glass, but who had the images burned on to their minds of someone they knew or loved who had been whole seconds before and was now sliced, torn, bludgeoned or broken.

In the blocks of flats leading up to Calle Los Romeros, the local police were evacuating the buildings. An old man in bloody pyjamas was being led by a boy, who had realized his importance. A young man holding a crimson-flashed towel to the side of his head stared through Falcón, his face horribly partitioned by rivulets of blood, coagulating with dust. He had his arm around his girlfriend, who appeared unhurt and was talking at full tilt into her mobile phone.

The air, more dust-filled by the moment, was still splintering to the sound of breaking glass as it fell from high shattered windows. Falcón called Ramírez again and told him to organize three or four buses to act as improvised ambulances to ferry the lightly wounded from all these blocks of apartments down the road to the hospital.

'The gas company have confirmed that they supply buildings in that area,' said Ramírez, 'but there's been no report of a leak and they ran a routine test on that block only last month.'

'For some reason this doesn't feel like a gas explosion,' said Falcón.

'We're getting reports that a pre-school behind the destroyed building has been badly damaged by flying debris and there are casualties.'

Falcón pressed on up through the walking wounded. There were still no signs of serious damage to buildings, but the people floating around, calling and looking for family members in the spaces at the foot of the emptying apartment blocks were phantasmal, dust-covered, not themselves. The light had turned strange, as the sun was scarfed by smoke and a reddish fog. There was a smell in the air, which was not immediately recognizable to anyone who didn't know war. It clogged the nostrils with powdered brick and concrete, raw sewage, open drains and a disgusting meatiness. The atmosphere was vibrant, but not with any discernible sound, although people were making noise – talking, coughing, vomiting and groaning – it was more of an airborne tinnitus, brought about by a collective human alarm at the proximity of death.

Lines of fire engines, lights flashing, were backed up all the way to Avenida San Lazaro. There wasn't a pane of intact glass in the apartment buildings on the other side of Calle Los Romeros. A bottle bank was sticking out of the side of one of the blocks like a huge green plug. A wall that ran down the street opposite the stricken building had been blown on to its back and cars were piled up in a garden, as if it was a scrapyard. The torn stumps of four trees lined the road. Other vehicles parked on Calle Los Romeros were buried under rubble: roofs crumpled, windscreens opaque, tyres blown out, wheel trims off. There were clothes strewn everywhere, as if there'd been a laundry drop from the sky. A length of chain-link fencing hung from a fourth-floor balcony.

Firemen had clambered up the nearest cascade of rubble and had their hoses trained on the two remaining sections of what had been a complete L-shaped building. What was now missing was a twenty-five-metre segment from the middle of it. The colossal explosion had brought down all eight floors of the block, to form a stack of reinforced concrete pancakes to a height of about six metres. Framed by the ragged remains of the eight floors of apartments, and just visible through the mist of falling dust, was the roof of the partially devastated pre-school and the apartment blocks beyond, whose façades were patched with black and gaping glassless windows. A fireman appeared on the edge of a broken room on the eighth floor and in the war-torn air made a sign to show that the building was now clear of people. A bed fell from the sixth floor, its frame crunched into the piled debris, while its mattress bounced off wildly in the direction of the pre-school.

On the other side of the rubble, further down Calle Los Romeros, was the Fire Chief's car but no sign of any officers. Falcón walked along the collapsed wall and made his way around the block to see what had happened to the pre-school. The end of the building closest to the explosion had lost two walls, part of the roof had collapsed and the rest was hanging, ready to drop. Firemen and civilians were propping the roof, while unblinking women stared on in appalled silence, hands holding their faces as if to stop them from dropping off in disbelief.

On the other side, at the entrance to the school, it was worse. Four small bodies lay side by side, their faces covered with school pinafores. A large group of men and women were trying to control two of the mothers of the dead children. Covered in dust they were like ghosts, fighting for the right to go back to the living. The women were screaming hysterically and clawing madly against hands trying to prevent them from reaching the inert bodies. Another woman had fainted and was lying on the ground, surrounded by people kneeling to protect her from the swaying and surging crowd. Falcón looked around for a teacher and saw a young woman sitting on a mat of broken glass, blood trickling down the side of her face, weeping uncontrollably, while a friend tried to console the inconsolable. A paramedic arrived to give her wounds some temporary dressing.

'Are you a teacher?' asked Falcón, of the woman's friend. 'Do you know where the mother of the fourth child is?'

The woman, dazed, looked across at the collapsed apartment block.

'She's in there somewhere,' she said, shaking her head.

Only firemen moved around inside the pre-school, their boots crunching over debris and glass. More props came in to support the shattered roof. The Fire Chief was in an undamaged classroom at the back of the school, giving a report to the Mayor's office on his mobile.

'All gas and electricity to the area has been cut off and the damaged building has been evacuated. Two fires have been brought under control,' he said. 'We've pulled four dead children out of the pre-school. Their classroom was in the direct path of the explosion and took its full force. So far we've had reports of three other deaths: two men and a woman who were walking along Calle Los Romeros when the explosion occurred. My men have also found a woman who seems to have died from a heart attack in one of the apartment blocks opposite the destroyed building. It's too difficult to say how many wounded there are at the moment.'

He listened for a moment longer and closed down the phone. Falcón showed his ID.

'You're here very early, Inspector Jefe,' said the Fire Chief.

'I was in the Forensic Institute. It sounded like a bomb from there. Is that what you think?'

'To do that sort of damage, there's no doubt in my mind that it was a bomb, and a very powerful one at that.'

'Any idea how many people were in that building?'

'I've got one of my officers working on that at the moment. There were at least seven,' he said. 'The only thing we can't be sure of is how many were in the mosque in the basement.'

'The mosque?'

'That's the other reason why I'm sure this was a

bomb,' said the Fire Chief. 'There was a mosque in the basement, with access from Calle Los Romeros. We think that morning prayers had just finished, but we're not sure if anyone had left. We're getting conflicting reports on that from the outside.'

6

Desperation had brought Consuelo to Calle Vidrio early. The children were being taken to school by her neighbour. Now she was sitting in her car outside Alicia Aguado's consulting room, getting cold feet about the emergency appointment she'd arranged only twenty-five minutes earlier. She walked the street to calm her nerves. She was not someone who had things wrong with her.

At precisely 8.30 a.m., having stared at the second hand of her watch, chipping away at the seconds – which showed her how obsessive she was becoming – she rang the doorbell. Dr Aguado was waiting for her, as she had been for many months. She was excited at the prospect of this new patient. Consuelo walked up the narrow stairs to the consulting room, which had been painted a pale blue and was kept at a constant temperature of 22°C.

Although Consuelo knew everything about Alicia Aguado, she let the clinical psychologist explain that she was now blind due to a degenerative disease called retinitis pigmentosa and that as a result of this disability

74

she had developed a unique technique of reading a patient's pulse.

'Why do you need to do that?' asked Consuelo, knowing the answer, but wanting to put off the moment when they got down to work.

'Because I'm blind I miss out on the most important indicators of the human body, which is physiognomy. We speak more to each other with our features and bodies than we do with our mouths. Think how little you would glean from a conversation just by hearing words. Only if someone was in an extreme state, such as fear or anxiety, would you understand what they were feeling, whereas if you have a face and body you pick up on a whole range of subtleties. You can tell the difference between someone who is lying, or exaggerating, someone who's bored, and someone who wants to go to bed with you. Reading the pulse, which I learnt from a Chinese doctor and have adapted to my needs, enables me to pick up on nuance.'

'That sounds like an intelligent way of saying that you're a human polygraph.'

'I don't just detect lies,' said Aguado. 'It's more to do with undercurrents. Translating feeling into language can defeat even the greatest of writers, so why should it be any easier for an ordinary person to tell me about their emotions, especially if they're in a confused state?'

'This is a beautiful room,' said Consuelo, already shying away from some of the words she'd heard in Aguado's explanation. Undercurrents reminded her of her fears, of being dragged out into the ocean to die of exhaustion alone in a vast heaving expanse.

'There was too much noise,' said Aguado. 'You know how it is in Seville. Noise was becoming so much of a distraction for me, in my state, that I had the room double-glazed and soundproofed. It used to be white, but I think my patients found white as intimidating as black. So I opted for tranquil blue. Let's sit down, shall we?'

They sat in the S-shaped lovers' seat, facing each other. She showed Consuelo the tape recorder in the armrest, explaining that it was the only way for her to review her consultations. Aguado asked her to introduce herself, give her age and any medication she was on so that she could check it was recording properly.

'Can you give me a brief medical history?'

'Since when?'

'Anything significant since you were born – operations, serious illnesses, children . . . that sort of thing.'

Consuelo tried to drink the tranquillity of the pale blue walls into her mind. She had been hoping for some miraculous surgical strike on her mental disturbances, a fabulous technique to yank open the tangled mess and smooth it out into comprehensible strands. In her turmoil it hadn't occurred to her that this was going to be a process, an intrusive process.

'You seem to be struggling with this question,' said Aguado.

'I'm just coming to terms with the fact that you're going to turn me inside out.'

'Nothing leaves this room,' said Aguado. 'We can't even be heard. The tapes are locked up in a safe in my office.'

'It's not that,' said Consuelo. 'I hate to vomit. I would rather sweat out my nausea than vomit up the problem. This is going to be mental vomiting.'

'Most people who arrive at my side are here because

of something intensely private, so private that it might even be a secret from themselves,' said Aguado. 'Mental health and physical health are not dissimilar. Untreated wounds fester and infect the whole body. Untreated lesions of the mind are no different. The only difficulty is that you can't just show me the infected cut. You might not know what, or where, it is. The only way for us to find out is by bringing things from the subconscious to the surface of the conscious mind. It's not vomiting. It's not expelling poison. You bring perhaps painful things to the surface, so that we can examine them, but they remain yours. If anything, it's *more* like sweating out your nausea than vomiting.'

'I've had two abortions,' said Consuelo, decisively. 'The first in 1980, the second in 1984. Both were performed in a London clinic. I have had three children. Ricardo in 1992, Matías in 1994 and Darío in 1998. Those are the only five occasions I have been in hospital.'

'Are you married?'

'Not any more. My husband died,' said Consuelo, stumbling over this first obstacle, used to obfuscation of the fact, rather than natural openness. 'He was murdered in 2001.'

'Was that a happy marriage?'

'He was thirty-four years older than me. I didn't know this at the time, but he married me because I reminded him physically of his first wife, who had committed suicide. I didn't want to marry him, but he was insistent. I only agreed when he said that he would give me children. Quite soon after the marriage he found out, or allowed himself to realize, that my likeness to his wife stopped at the physical. We still stayed

77

together. We respected each other, especially in business. He was a diligent father. But as for loving me, making me happy . . . no.'

'Did you hear that?' asked Aguado. 'Something outside. A big noise, like an explosion.'

'I didn't hear anything.'

'I know about your husband's case, of course,' said Aguado. 'It was truly terrible. That must have been very traumatic for you and the children.'

'It was. But it's not directly linked to why I'm sitting here,' said Consuelo. 'That investigation was necessarily intrusive. I was a prime suspect. He was a wealthy, influential man. I had a lover. The police believed I had a motive. My life was turned inside out by the investigation. Nasty details of my past were revealed.'

'Such as?'

'I had appeared in a pornographic movie when I was seventeen to raise money to pay for my first abortion.'

Aguado forced Consuelo to relive that ugly slice of her life in great detail and didn't let her stop until she'd explained the circumstances of the next pregnancy, with a duke's son, which had led to the second abortion.

'What do you think of pornography?' asked Alicia.

'I abhor it,' said Consuelo. 'I especially abhorred my need to be involved in it, in order to find the money to terminate a pregnancy.'

'What do you think pornography is?'

'The filming of the biological act of sex.'

'Is that all?'

'It is sex without emotion.'

'You described quite strong emotions when you were telling me —'

'Of disgust and revulsion, yes.'

'For your partners in the movie?'

'No, no, not at all,' said Consuelo. 'We were all in the same boat, us girls. And the men needed us to perform. It's not a highly sexually charged atmosphere on a porn set. We were all high on dope, to help us get over what we were doing.'

Consuelo's enthusiasm for her account waned. She wasn't getting to the point.

'So who were these strong feelings of anger aimed at?' asked Aguado.

'Myself,' said Consuelo, hoping that this partial truth might be enough.

'When I asked you what pornography was, I don't believe you were telling me what *you* actually thought,' said Aguado. 'You were giving me a socially acceptable version. Try answering that question again.'

'It's sex without love,' said Consuelo, hammering the chair. 'It's the *antithesis* of love.'

'The antithesis of love is hate.'

'It's self-hate.'

'What else?'

'It's the desecration of sex.'

'What do you think of men and women being filmed having sex with multiple partners?' asked Aguado.

'It's perverted.'

'What else?'

'What do you mean, "what else"? I don't know *what else* you want.'

'How often have you thought about the movie since it came to light in your husband's murder investigation?'

'I forgot about it.'

79

'Until today?'

'What's that supposed to mean?'

'This isn't a social situation, Sra Jiménez.'

'I realize *that*.'

'You mustn't be concerned with what I think of you in that respect,' said Aguado.

'But I don't know what you're trying to get me to admit.'

'Why are we talking about pornography?'

'It was something that came to light in my husband's murder investigation.'

'I asked you whether your husband's murder had been traumatic,' said Aguado.

'I see.'

'What do you see?'

'That the movie coming to light was more traumatic for me than my husband's death.'

'Not necessarily. It was bound up in a traumatic event, and in that highly emotionally charged period it made its mark on you.'

Consuelo struggled in silence. The tangled mess was not unravelling but becoming even more confused.

'You've made appointments with me several times recently and you've never appeared for them,' said Aguado. 'Why did you come this morning?'

'I love my children,' said Consuelo. 'I love my children so much it hurts.'

'Where does it hurt?' asked Aguado, leaping on to this new revelation.

'You've never had children?'

Alicia Aguado shrugged.

'It hurts me in the top of my stomach, around my diaphragm.'

'Why does it hurt?'

'Can't you ever just accept something?' said Consuelo. 'I love them. It hurts.'

'We're here to examine your inner life. I can't feel it or see it. All I have to go on is how you express yourself.'

'And the pulse thing?'

'That's what raises the questions,' said Aguado. 'What you say and what I feel in your blood don't always match up.'

'Are you telling me I *don't* love my children?'

'No, I'm asking you why you say it hurts. What is causing you the pain?'

'*Joder!* It's the fucking love that hurts, you stupid bitch,' said Consuelo, tearing her wrist away, ripping her blabbing pulse out from under those questioning fingertips. 'I'm sorry. I'm really sorry. That was unforgivable.'

'Don't be sorry,' said Aguado. 'This is no cocktail party.'

'You're telling me,' said Consuelo. 'Look, I've always been very firm about telling the truth. My children will confirm that.'

'This is a different type of truth.'

'There is only *one* truth,' said Consuelo, with missionary zeal.

'There's the real truth, and the presentable truth,' said Aguado. 'They're often quite close together, but for a few emotional details.'

'You've got me wrong there, Doctor. I'm not like that. I've seen things, I've done things and I've faced up to them all.'

'That *is* why you're here.'

'You're calling me a liar and a coward. You're telling me I don't know who I am.'

'I'm asking questions, and you're doing your best to answer them.'

'But you've just told me that what I'm saying and what you're feeling in my pulse don't match. Therefore, you are calling me a liar.'

'I think we've had enough for today,' said Aguado. 'That's a lot of ground to have covered in the first session. I'd like to see you again very soon. Is this a good time of day for you? The morning or late afternoon is probably the best time in the restaurant business.'

'You think I'm coming back for any more of this shit?' said Consuelo, heading for the door, swinging her bag over her shoulder. 'Think again . . . blind bitch!'

She slammed the door on the way out and nearly went over on her heel in the cobbled street. She got into her car, jammed the keys into the ignition, but didn't start the engine. She hung on to the steering wheel, as if it was the only thing that would stop her falling off the edge of her sanity. She cried. She cried until it hurt in exactly the same place as it did when she was watching her children sleeping.

Angel and Manuela were sitting out on the roof terrace in the early-morning sunshine, having breakfast. Manuela sat in a white towelling robe examining her toes. Angel blinked with irritation as he read one of his articles in the *ABC*.

'They've cut a whole paragraph,' said Angel. 'Some stupid sub-editor is making my journalism look like the work of a fool.'

'I can hear myself getting fat,' said Manuela, barely thinking, her whole being consumed by the business that was to take place later that morning. 'I'm going to have to spend the rest of my life in a tracksuit.'

'I'm wasting my time,' said Angel. 'I'm just messing about, writing drivel for idiots. No wonder they cut it.'

'I'm going to paint my nails,' said Manuela. 'What do you think? Pink or red? Or something wild to distract people from my bottom?'

'That's it,' said Angel, tossing the newspaper across the terrace. 'I'm finished with this shit.'

And that was when they heard it: a distant, but significant, boom. They looked at each other, all immediate concerns gone from their minds. Manuela couldn't stop herself from saying the obvious.

'What the hell was that?'

'That,' said Angel, getting to his feet so suddenly that the chair collapsed beneath him, 'was a large explosion.'

'But where?'

'The sound came from the north.'

'Oh shit, Angel! Shit, shit, shit, shit, shit!'

'What?' said Angel, expecting to see her with red nail polish all over her foot.

'It can't possibly have slipped your mind already,' said Manuela. 'We've been up half the night talking about it. The two properties in the Plaza Moravia – which is north of where we're standing now.'

'It wasn't *that* close,' said Angel. 'That was outside the city walls.'

'That's the thing about journalists,' said Manuela, 'they're so used to having their fingers on the pulse that they think they know everything, even how far away an explosion is.'

'I'd have said . . . Oh my God. Do you think that was in the Estación de Santa Justa?'

'That's east,' she said, pointing vaguely over the rooftops.

'North is the Parliament building,' he said, looking at his watch. 'There won't be anybody there at this time.'

'Apart from a few expendable cleaners,' said Manuela.

Angel stood in front of the TV, flicking from channel to channel, until he found Canal Sur.

'We have some breaking news of a large explosion to the north of Seville . . . somewhere in the area of El Cerezo. Eyewitnesses say that an apartment block has been completely destroyed and a nearby pre-school has been badly damaged. We have no reports of the cause of the explosion or the number of casualties.'

'El Cerezo?' said Angel. 'What's in El Cerezo?'

'Nothing,' said Manuela. 'Cheap apartment blocks. It's probably a gas explosion.'

'You're right. It's a residential area.'

'Not every loud noise you hear has to be a bomb.'

'After March 11th and the London bombings, our minds move in natural directions,' said Angel, opening up a street map of Seville.

'Well, you're always wanting something to happen and now it has. You'd better find out if it was gas or terrorism. But, whatever you do, Angel, don't give –'

'El Cerezo is two kilometres from here,' he said, cutting through her rising hysteria. 'You said it yourself, it's a cheap residential area. It's got nothing to do with what you're trying to sell in the Plaza Moravia.'

'If that was a terrorist bomb, it doesn't matter where it went off . . . the whole city will be nervous. One of my buyers is a foreigner making an investment. Investors react to this kind of thing. Ask me, if you like – I *am* one.'

'Did the Madrid property market crash after March 11th?' asked Angel. 'Keep calm, Manuela. It was probably gas.'

'The bomb could have detonated accidentally while they were preparing it,' she said. 'They might have blown themselves up because they realized that they were about to be raided by the police.'

'Call Javier,' said Angel, stroking the back of her neck. 'He'll know something.'

Falcón called his immediate boss, the Jefe de Brigada de Policía Judicial, Comisario Pedro Elvira, to give his initial report that the Fire Chief was almost certain this level of destruction was caused by a significant bomb, and gave the number of casualties so far.

Elvira had just come out of a meeting with *his* boss, Seville's most senior policeman, the Jefe Superior de la Policía de Sevilla, Comisario Andrés Lobo, who had appointed him to lead the entire investigative operation. He also confirmed that the Magistrado Juez Decano de Sevilla had just appointed Esteban Calderón as the Juez de Instrucción in charge of directing the investigation. Three companies had been contacted to supply demolition crews to start removing the rubble and to work with rescue teams, who were already on their way, to try to find any survivors as quickly as possible.

Falcón made a number of requests: aerial photography, before the huge crime scene became too contaminated by the rescue and demolition operation. He also asked for a large police presence to cordon off nearly a square kilometre around the building, so that they could investigate every vehicle in the vicinity. If it was a bomb, it had to have been transported and the vehicle could still be there. When they started searching suspect vehicles they would also need a team of forensics and a unit from the bomb squad. Elvira confirmed everything back to him and hung up.

The Fire Chief was a man in his moment. He'd trained for this terrible day and brought the immediate calamity under control in less than ninety minutes. He accompanied Falcón to the edge of the destruction. On the way he ordered a crew of firemen to stop work on supporting the roof of the destroyed classroom so that the bomb squad could see how the explosion had affected the building. He talked Falcón through the architecture of the destroyed apartment block and how enormous the explosion must have been to blow out the four main supporting pillars for that section. The effect of that would have brought the sudden and phenomenal weight of all the reinforced concrete floors on to the skin walls between each storey. There would have been an accumulative weight and acceleration as each level fell from a greater and greater height.

'Nobody could have survived that collapse,' he said. 'We're praying for miracles here.'

'Why are you so certain that this couldn't have been a gas explosion?'

'Apart from the fact that there's been no reported leak, and we've only had to deal with two small fires, the mosque in the basement is in daily use. Gas is heavier than air and would accumulate at the lowest point. A large enough quantity of gas couldn't have accumulated without anybody noticing,' he said. 'Added to that, the gas would have had to collect in a big enough space before exploding. Its power would be dissipated. Our main problem would have been incendiary, rather than destruction. There would have been a massive fireball, which would have scorched the whole area. There would have been burns victims. A bomb explodes from a small, confined source. It therefore has far more concentrated destructive power. Only a very large bomb, or several smaller bombs, could have taken out those reinforced concrete supporting pillars. Most of the dead and injured we've seen so far have been hit by flying debris and glass. All the windows in the area have been blown out. It's all consistent with a bomb blast.'

At the edge of the destruction the light was bruised and sickly yellow. The pulverized brick and concrete formed a fine dust, which clogged the throat and nostrils with the stench of decay. From within the stacked floors came the repetitive, desperate sounds of mobile phone jingles, the same customized tunes begging to be answered. Here, rather than being an irritant, they had personality. The Fire Chief shook his head.

'It's the worst thing,' he said, 'listening to someone else's hope fading away.'

Falcón almost jumped as his own mobile vibrated against his thigh.

'Manuela,' he said, walking away from the Fire Chief.

'Are you all right, little brother?' she asked.

'Yes, but I'm busy.'

'I know,' she said. 'Just tell me one thing. Was it a bomb?'

'We've had no confirmation –'

'I don't want the official communiqué,' she said. 'I'm your sister.'

'I don't want Angel running off to the *ABC* with a quote from the Inspector Jefe at the scene.'

'This is for my ears only.'

'Don't be ridiculous.'

'Just tell me, Javier.'

'We think it was a bomb.'

'Fuck.'

Falcón hung up in a fury without saying goodbye. Men, women and children had died and been injured. Families had been destroyed, along with homes and possessions. But Manuela still needed to know which way the property market was going to tip.

7

A figure sprinted between Falcón and the Fire Chief as he closed down his mobile. The man stumbled into the rubble at the foot of the fallen building, picked himself up and ran at the stacked pancakes of the re-inforced concrete floors. His scale was strangely dimin-ished by the vastness of the collapse. He seemed like a puppet as he dithered to the left and right, trying to find a purchase point in the tangle of cracked concrete, bristling steel rods, ruptured netting and shattered brick.

The Fire Chief shouted at him. He didn't hear. He plunged his hands into the wreckage, swung his body up and hooked his leg over a thick steel rod, but he was a horribly human mixture of crazed strength over-whelmed by futility.

By the time they got to him he was hanging help-less, his palms already torn and bloody, his face distorted by the rawness of his pain. They lifted him off his ghastly perch, like soldiers removing a comrade from the wire of the front line. No sooner had they got him down than he recovered his strength and lunged at the building once more. Falcón had to tackle him around the legs to hold him back. They scrabbled over the rubble, like an ancient articulated insect, until Falcón managed to crawl up the man's body and clasp his arms to his chest.

'You can't go in there,' he said, his voice rasping from the dust.

The man grunted and flexed his arms against Falcón's embrace. His mouth was wide open, his eyes stared into the mangled mess of the building and sweat beaded in fat drops on his filthy face.

'Who do you know who is in there?' asked Falcón.

On the back of the man's grunting came two words – wife, daughter.

'Which floor?' asked the Fire Chief.

The man looked up at them blinking, as if this question demanded some complicated differential calculus.

'Gloria,' said the man. 'Lourdes.'

'But which floor?' asked the Fire Chief.

The man's head went limp, all fight gone. Falcón released him and rolled him on to his back.

'Do you know anybody else in there, apart from Gloria and Lourdes?' asked Falcón.

The man's head listed to one side, and his dark eyes took in the damaged end of the pre-school. He sat up, got to his feet and trod robotically through the rubble and household detritus between the apartment block and the pre-school. Falcón followed. The man stood at the point where there should have been a wall. The classroom was a turmoil of broken furniture and shards of glass, and on the far wall fluttering in a breeze were children's paintings – big suns, mad smiles, hair standing on end.

The man's feet crunched through the glass. He tripped and fell heavily over a twisted desk, but righted himself immediately and made for the paintings. He pulled one off the wall and looked at it with the intensity of a collector judging a masterpiece. There was a tree, a sun, a high building and four people – two big, two small. In the bottom right-hand corner was a name written in an adult hand – Pedro. The man folded it carefully and put it inside his shirt.

The three men went into the main corridor of the school and out through the entrance. The local police had arrived and were trying to clear a path for the ambulance to remove the four bodies of the dead children taken from the destroyed classroom. Two of the mothers kneeling at the feet of their children gave a hysterical howl at this latest development. The third mother had already been taken away.

A woman with a thick white bandage on the side of her face, through which the blood underneath was just beginning to bloom, recognized the man.

'Fernando,' she said.

The man turned to her, but didn't recognize her.

'I'm Marta, Pedro's teacher,' she said.

Fernando had lost the power of speech. He took the painting out of his shirt and pointed at the smallest figure. Marta's motor reflexes seemed to malfunction and she couldn't swallow what was in her throat, nor articulate what was in her mind. Instead her face just caved in and she only managed to squeeze out a sound of such brutality and ugliness that it left Fernando's chest shuddering. It was a sound uncontrolled by any civilizing influence. It was grief in its purest form, before its pain had been made less acute by time or more

91

poignant by poetry. It was a dark, guttural, heaving clot of emotion.

Fernando was not affronted. He folded the painting up and put it back in his shirt. Falcón led him by the arm to the four small bodies. The ambulance was backing up, the rest of the crowd had been squeezed out of the scene. Two paramedics appeared with two body bags each. They worked quickly because they knew the situation would be better with those pitiful bodies removed. Falcón held Fernando around the shoulders as the paramedics uncovered each body and placed it in a body bag. He had to remind Fernando to breathe. At the third body Fernando's knees buckled and Falcón lowered him to the ground, where he fell forward on to all fours and crawled around, like a poisoned dog looking for a place to die. One of the paramedics shouted and pointed. A TV cameraman had come around the back, through the pre-school, and was filming the bodies. He turned and ran before anybody could react.

The ambulance moved off. The ghostly crowd surged after it and gave up, with a final spasm of grief, before dissolving into groups, with the bereaved women supported from all sides. Television journalists and their cameramen tried to force their way in to talk to the women. They were rebuffed. Falcón pulled Fernando to his feet, pushed him back into the pre-school out of sight, and went to find a policeman to keep journalists away.

Outside a journalist had found a young guy in his twenties, with a couple of bloody nicks in his cheek, who'd been there when the bomb exploded. The camera was right in his face, inches away, the proximity giving the pictures their urgency.

'. . . straight after it happened, I mean, the noise . . . you just can't believe the loudness of that noise, it was so loud I couldn't breathe, it was like . . .'

'What was it like?' asked the journalist, an eager young woman, stabbing the microphone back into his face. 'Tell us. Tell Spain what it was like.'

'It was like the noise took away all the air.'

'What was the first thing you noticed after the explosion, after the noise?'

'Silence,' he said. 'Just a deathly quiet. And, I don't know whether this was in my head or it actually happened, I heard bells ringing . . .'

'Church bells?'

'Yes, church bells, but they were all crazy, as if the shock waves of the explosion were making them ring, you know, at random. It made me sick to hear it. It was as if everything had gone wrong with the world, and nothing would be the same.'

The rest was lost in the clatter and thump of a helicopter's rotor blades, thrashing away at the dust in the air. It went up higher, to take in the whole scene. This was the aerial photography Falcón had ordered up.

He posted a policeman at the entrance of the school, but found that Fernando had disappeared. He crossed the corridor to the wrecked classroom. Empty. He called Ramírez as he crashed through the broken furniture.

'Where are you?' asked Falcón.

'We've just arrived. We're on Calle Los Romeros.'

'Is Cristina with you?'

'We're all here. The whole squad.'

'All of you come round to the pre-school now.'

Fernando was back at the wall of rubble and collapsed floors. He threw himself at it like a madman. He tore at the concrete, bricks, window frames and hurled them behind him.

'. . . rescue teams working on this side,' roared Ramírez, over the noise of the helicopter. 'There are dogs in the wreckage.'

'Get over here.'

Fernando had grabbed at the steel netting of a shattered reinforced concrete floor. He had his feet braced against the rubble. His neck muscles stood out and his carotid arteries appeared as thick as cord. Falcón pulled him off and they fought for some moments, tripping and floundering about in the dust and rubble until they were ghosts of their former selves.

'Have you got Gloria's phone number?' roared Falcón.

They were panting in the choking atmosphere, their sweating faces caked with grey, white and brown dust, which swirled around them from the chopper's blades.

The question transfixed Fernando. Despite hearing all these mobile phones ringing, his mind was so paralysed with shock, he hadn't thought of his own. He ripped it out of his pocket. He squeezed life into the starter button. The helicopter moved off, leaving an immense silence.

Fernando blinked, his brain fluttering like torn flags, trying to remember his PIN. It came to him and he thumbed in Gloria's number. He stood up from his kneeling position and walked towards the wreckage. He held a hand up as if demanding silence from the world. From his left came the faint, tinny sound of some Cuban piano.

'That's her,' he roared, moving left. 'She was on this side of the building when . . . when I last saw her.'

Falcón got to his feet and made a futile attempt to dust himself down just as his homicide squad turned up. He stayed them with his hand and moved towards the tinkling piano, which he recognized as a song called 'Lágrimas Negras' – Black Tears.

'She's there!' roared Fernando. 'She's in there!'

Baena, a junior detective from Falcón's squad, ran back and fetched a rescue team with a dog. The team pinpointed the spot from where the ringing tone was coming and managed to get Fernando to tell them that his wife and daughter had been on the fifth floor. They gave him steady looks when he released that information. In the face of his radiant hope not one of them had the heart to tell him that the fall, with three storeys coming down on top, meant that, at this moment, they were praying only.

'She's in there,' he said, to their still, expressionless faces. 'That mobile is always with her. She's a sales rep. "Lágrimas Negras" was her favourite song.'

Falcón nodded to Cristina Ferrera and they guided Fernando back to the pre-school and got a nurse to clean him up and dress his cuts. Falcón called the homicide squad into the school latrines. He washed his hands and face and looked at them in the mirror.

'This is going to be the most complicated investigation that any of us have ever been involved in, and that includes me,' said Falcón. 'Nothing is straightforward in terrorist attacks. We know that from what happened on March 11th in Madrid. There are going to be a lot of people involved – the CNI's intelligence agents, the CGI's antiterrorist squad, the bomb disposal

95

teams and us – and that's just on the investigative side. What we've got to do is keep it clear in our minds what we, as the homicide squad, are trying to achieve. I've already asked for a police cordon to keep the site clear for us.'

'They're in place,' said Ramírez. 'They're working on getting the journalists out.'

Falcón turned to face them, shaking his wet hands.

'By now you all know that there was a mosque in the basement of that block. Our job is not to speculate on what happened and why. Our job is to find out who went into that mosque, and who came out, and what went on inside it in the last twenty-four hours, and then forty-eight hours, and so on. We do that by talking to every possible witness we can find. Our other crucial task is to find out about every vehicle in the vicinity. The bomb was big. It would have had to be transported to this place. If that vehicle is still here, we have to find it.

'At the moment the first task is going to be difficult, with all the occupants of the apartments evacuated from their buildings. So our priority is to identify all vehicles and their owners. José Luis will divide you up and you will search every sector, starting with cars closest to the collapsed building. Cristina, you'll stay with me for the moment.

'And remember, everybody here is suffering in some way, whether they've lost somebody or seen them injured, whether they've had their home destroyed or their windows smashed. You've got a heavy workload and you're going to be under a lot of pressure, with or without the media on your backs. You'll get more information by being sensitive and understanding than by treating this as the usual process. You're all good people, which is why you're in the homicide squad – now go out there and find out what happened.'

They filed out. Ferrera stayed behind. Falcón washed his hair under the tap and then wiped his face and hands.

'His name is Fernando. His wife and daughter were in the collapsed apartment block, his son was one of the children killed in the blast. Find out if he has any other family and, if not, any close friends. Not anybody will do. He left home after his breakfast to find out, half an hour later, that he's lost everything. When it comes home to him, he's going to lose his mind.'

'And you want me to stay with him?'

'I can't afford that. I want you to make sure he's safely delivered into the hands of a trauma team, who should be along any minute. He needs his predicament explained, he's lost the ability to articulate. He'll want to stay here until the bodies are found. But don't lose track of him. I want to know where he ends up.'

They left the latrines. A bomb squad team was picking its way through the shattered classroom, like mineral fossickers looking for valuable rocks. They filled polypropylene sacks with their finds. There were two more teams outside, working furiously so that the machinery could move in to start the demolition task and the search for survivors.

Cristina Ferrera went into the classroom where the nurse was just finishing dressing Fernando's cuts. She knew why Falcón had chosen her for this job. The nurse was doing her best with Fernando, but he wasn't

97

responding, his brain was teeming with bigger, darker fish. The nurse finished and packed up. Cristina asked her to send someone from a trauma team as soon as possible. She sat on a chair by the blackboard, at some distance from Fernando. She didn't want to crowd him, even though it was obvious that he was living inside his head at an intensity that excluded the outside world. Grief darkened, as quickly as hope lightened, his face, like clouds passing over fields.

'Who are *you*?' he asked, after some minutes, as if noticing her for the first time.

'I'm a policewoman. My name is Cristina Ferrera.'

'There was a man before. Who was he?'

'That was my boss, Javier Falcón. He's the Inspector Jefe of the homicide squad.'

'He's got some work on his hands.'

'He's a good man,' said Ferrera. 'An unusual man. He'll get to the bottom of it.'

'We all know who it is, though, don't we?'

'Not yet.'

'The Moroccans.'

'It's too early to say.'

'You ask around. We've all thought about it. Ever since March 11th we've watched them going in there and we've been waiting.'

'Into the mosque, you mean? The mosque in the basement.'

'That's right.'

'They're not all Moroccans who go to mosques, you know. Plenty of Spaniards have converted to Islam.'

'I work in construction,' he said, uninterested in her balanced approach. 'I put together buildings like that. Much better buildings than that. I work with steel.'

'In Seville?'

'Yes, I build apartments for rich young professionals . . . that's what I'm told anyway.'

Fernando's head had been turned upside down and now he was trying to put the furniture straight. Except that, occasionally, he noticed the furniture's emptiness and it tipped his mind back into the abyss of loss and grief. He tried to talk about building work but got lost in moments of imagination as he saw his wife and daughter falling through steel and concrete. He wanted to get out of himself, out of his body and head and into . . . where? Where could the mind go for respite? A helicopter battering the air overhead knocked his thoughts into another pattern.

'Do you have children?' he asked.

'A boy and a girl,' she said.

'How old?'

'The boy's sixteen. The girl's fourteen.'

'Good kids,' he said; not a question, more of a hope.

'They're both being difficult at the moment,' she said. 'Their father died about three years ago. It's not been easy for them.'

'I'm sorry,' he said, but wanting her tragedy to bury his own for a while. 'How did he die?'

'He died of a rare type of cancer.'

'That's hard for your kids. Fathers are good for them at that age,' he said. 'They like to try things out on their mothers to give themselves the confidence to rebel against the world. That's what Gloria told me, anyway. They need fathers to show them it's not as easy as they think.'

'You might be right.'

'Gloria says I'm a good father.'

'Your wife . . .'

'Yes, my wife,' he said.

'Can you tell me about your own kids?' she asked.

He couldn't. There were no words for them. He measured them out with a hand up from the floor, he pointed out of the window at the destroyed apartment block, and finally he pulled the painting out from his shirt. That said it all – sticks and triangles, a tall rectangle with windows, a round green tree and behind it a massive orange sun in a blue sky.

A colossal crane arrived, preceded by a bulldozer, which cleared the land in between the destroyed block and the pre-school. Two tipper trucks manoeuvred around the back of the crane and a digger began to scoop rubble and dump it in the tippers. In the cleared land the crane settled its feet and a team of men in yellow hard hats began preparing the rig.

Around the front of the building, on Calle Los Romeros, a change of clothes had arrived from the Jefatura for Falcón. The rest of the homicide squad were busy working with the local police, identifying vehicles and their owners. Comisario Elvira had turned up in full uniform and was being given a tour of the site by the Fire Chief. As he moved around, his assistant called all the team leaders involved in the operation to a meeting in one of the classrooms in the pre-school. As the entourage headed for the pre-school a woman approached Elvira and gave him a list with twelve names on it.

'And who are these people?' asked Elvira.

'They are the names of all the men in the mosque at the time of the explosion not including the Imam, Abdelkrim Benaboura,' she said. 'My name is Esperanza.

I'm Spanish. My partner, who is also Spanish, was in the mosque. I represent the wives, mothers and girlfriends of these men. We are in hiding. The women, especially the Moroccan women, are scared that people may think that their husbands and sons were in some way responsible for what has happened. There's a mobile number on the back of the list. We would ask you to call us when you have some news of their . . . of anything.'

She moved away, and the pressure of time and lack of personnel meant that Elvira let her go unfollowed. Calderón made his way through the crowd to Falcón.

'I didn't realize it was you, Javier,' he said, shaking him by the hand. 'How did you get into that state?'

'I had to stop someone from throwing himself into the wreckage to rescue his wife and daughter.'

'So, this is the big one,' said Calderón, not bothering to engage with what Falcón had said. 'It's finally happened to us.'

They continued to the school, where the police, judges, fire brigade, bomb squad, rescue services, trauma units, medical services and demolition gangs were all represented. Elvira made it clear that nobody was allowed to say a word until he had delivered the plan of action. To focus their attention he asked the leader of the bomb squad to give a brief report on the initial analyses of fragments from the blast. They showed that the apartment block had been devastated by a bomb of extraordinary power, most probably situated in the basement of that section of the building, and whose explosive was probably of military, rather than commercial, quality. This expert opinion silenced the assembled company completely and Elvira was able to hammer out a co-ordinated plan in about forty minutes.

At the end of the meeting Ramírez headed Falcón off as he was making for the latrines to change his clothes.

'We've got something,' he said.

'Talk me through it while I change.'

As soon as he was dressed, Falcón found Comisario Elvira and Juez Calderón, and asked Ramírez to repeat what he'd just told him.

'In the immediate vicinity of the building, excluding vehicles buried in the rubble, we've found three stolen cars plus this van,' said Ramírez. 'It's parked right outside the pre-school here. It's a Peugeot Partner, registered in Madrid. There's a copy of the Koran on the front seat. We can't see in the back because it's a closed van and the rear windows have been shattered, but the owner of the vehicle is a man called Mohammed Soumaya.'

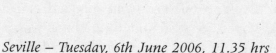

8

Seville – Tuesday, 6th June 2006, 11.35 hrs

The car park was directly behind the destroyed building and next to the pre-school. There were some trees, which provided a canopy to a sitting area near Calle Blanca Paloma on one side and a five-storey apartment block on the other. There was only one access road to the car park. While Calderón, Elvira, Falcón and Ramírez made for the Peugeot Partner, Elvira's assistant logged on to the police terror suspects list and entered Mohammed Soumaya's details. He was in the lowest risk category, which meant that he had no known connections to any body, organization or persons with either terror or radical Islamic background. The only reason he was on the list was that he fitted the most basic terrorist profile: under forty years of age, a devout Muslim and single. Elvira's assistant entered the names from the list of all the men in the mosque at the time of the explosion, which had been given by the Spanish woman, Esperanza. There was no Mohammed Soumaya among them. He patched the names through to the CNI – the Spanish intelligence agency.

Two breakdown vehicles were working in the car

park to remove cars whose owners had been identified and screened. Most of these cars had windows smashed and bodywork damage from flying debris. The Peugeot Partner's two rear windows were opaque with shattered glass and the rear doors were dented. The side windows were clear and the windscreen, which had been facing away from the explosion, was intact. The copy of the Koran, a new Spanish edition, was visible on the front passenger seat. Two forensics in white hooded boiler suits and latex gloves were standing by. There was a discussion about booby traps and a bomb squad team was called over, along with a dog handler. The dog found nothing interesting around the car. The underside and engine compartment were inspected and found clear. The bomb squad man picked the glass out of one of the smashed rear windows and inspected inside. The rear doors were opened and shots taken of the empty interior and its carpeted floor. A fine, crystalline, white powder, which covered an area of about 30 cm by 20 cm, had been spilled on the floor. The excited sniffer dog leapt in and immediately sat down by the powder. One of the forensics took a hand-held vacuum cleaner with a clear plastic flask attached and hoovered up the powder. The flask was removed from the vacuum cleaner, capped and given an evidence number.

The forensics moved round to the front of the car and bagged the new copy of the Koran, whose spine was unbroken. In the glove compartment they found another copy of the Koran. This was a heavily used Spanish translation, with copious notes in the margins; it proved to be exactly the same edition as the one found on the front seat. This was bagged, as were the vehicle documents. Falcón took a note of the ISBN and bar codes of both books. Under the passenger seat was an empty mineral water bottle and a black cotton sack, which contained a carefully folded green-and-white sash whose length was covered in Arabic writing. There was also a black hood with eye and mouth holes.

'Let's not get too excited until we've had an analysis of that powder in the back,' said Calderón. 'His occupation is "shop owner", it could just as easily be sugar.'

'Not if my dog sat down next to it,' said the bomb squad man. 'He's never wrong.'

'We'd better get in touch with Madrid and have someone visit Mohammed Soumaya's home and business premises,' said Falcón, and Ramírez moved off to make the call. 'We want detail about his movements over the last forty-eight hours, as well.'

'You're going to have a job on your hands just to find all these people who had a view of this car park, and the front and rear of the destroyed building,' said Calderón. 'As the bomb squad guy said, it was a big bomb, which means a lot of explosive arrived here, possibly in small lots and maybe from a number of different suppliers, and at different times.'

'We're going to need to know whether the mosque, or any of the people in the mosque, were the subject of surveillance by the CGI's antiterrorist squad or the CNI's intelligence agents and, if they were, we'd like that information,' said Falcón. 'And, by the way, where are they? I didn't see anybody from the CGI in that meeting.'

'The CNI are on their way down here now,' said Elvira.

'And the CGI?' asked Calderón.

'They're in lockdown,' said Elvira, quietly.

'What does that mean?' said Calderón.

'It will be explained to us when the CNI get here,' said Elvira.

'How much longer will it be before the fire brigade and the bomb squad can declare all these apartment blocks surrounding the destroyed building safe?' asked Falcón. 'At least if people can come back to their homes we've got a chance of building up our information quickly.'

'They know that,' said Elvira, 'and they've told me that they should be letting people back in within the next few hours, as long as they don't find anything else. In the meantime a contact number's been issued to the press, TV and radio for people to call in with information.'

'Except that they don't know of the Peugeot Partner's importance yet,' said Falcón. 'We're not going to get anywhere until people get back into their apartments.'

The Mayor, who'd been stuck in traffic as the city had ground to a halt, finally arrived in the car park. He was joined by ministers of the Andalucían Parliament, who had just come from the hospital where they'd been filmed talking to some of the victims. A gaggle of journalists had been allowed through the police cordon and they gathered around the officials, while camera crews set up their equipment, with the destruction providing the devastating backdrop. Elvira went across to the Mayor to give his situation report and was intercepted by his own assistant. They talked. Elvira pointed him across to Falcón.

'Only three of the twelve names given to us on that list appear on the terror suspect database,' said the assistant, 'and they're all in the lowest risk category.

Five of the twelve were over sixty-five. Morning prayers isn't such a popular time with the young, as most people have to get to work.'

'Not exactly the classic profile of a terrorist cell,' said Falcón. 'But then we don't know who else was in there yet.'

'How many under the age of thirty-five?' asked Calderón.

'Four,' said the assistant, 'and of those, two are brothers, one of whom is severely disabled in a wheel-chair, and another is a Spanish convert called Miguel Botín.'

'And the remaining three?'

'Four, including the Imam, who isn't on the list the woman gave us. He's fifty-five and the other three are in their forties. Two of them are claiming disability benefit from the state after suffering industrial accidents, and the third is another Spanish convert.'

'Well, they don't sound like a special forces unit, do they?' said Calderón.

'There is one interesting point. The Imam is on the terror suspect database. He's been in Spain since September 2004, arriving from Tunis.'

'And before that?'

'That's the point. I don't have the clearance for that level of information. Maybe the Comisario does,' he said, and went to rejoin the media scrum around the Mayor.

'How can somebody be in a low-risk category and yet have a higher level of clearance for his history?' asked Ramírez.

'Let's look at the certainties, or the almost certainties,' said Juez Calderón. 'We have a bomb explosion,

whose epicentre seems to be the mosque in the basement of the building. We have a van belonging to
Mohammed Soumaya, a low-risk category terrorist –
who we are not sure was in the building at the time
of the blast. His van bears traces of explosive, according
to the bomb squad dog. We have a list of twelve people
in the mosque at the time, plus the Imam. Only three,
plus the Imam, make it on to a list of low-risk category terror suspects. We are investigating the deaths of
four children in the pre-school and three people outside
the apartment block at the time of the explosion.
Anything else?'

'The hood, the sash, the two copies of the Koran,'
said Ramírez.

'We should get all those notes in the margins of the
used copy of the Koran looked at by an expert,' said
Calderón. 'Now, what are the questions we want
answered?'

'Did Mohammed Soumaya drive this van here? If
not, who did? If that powder is confirmed as explosive
then what was it, why was it being gathered here, and
why did it detonate?' said Falcón. 'While we wait to
hear from Madrid about Soumaya we'll build up a
picture of what happened in and around this mosque
over the last week. We can start by asking people
whether they remember this van arriving, how many
people were in it, did they see it being unloaded and
so on. Can we get a shot of Soumaya?'

Ramírez, who was on the phone again, trying to sort
out someone to look at the copy of the Koran, nodded
and twirled an index finger to show that he was on to
it. A policewoman came from the wreckage site and
informed Calderón that the first body in the collapsed

building had been found – an old woman on the eighth floor. They agreed to reconvene in a couple of hours. Ramírez came off the phone as Cristina Ferrera arrived from the pre-school.

It was agreed that Ramírez would continue working on the vehicle identification with Sub-Inspector Pérez, Serrano and Baena. Falcón and Cristina Ferrera would start trying to find the occupants of the five-storey apartment building with the best view of the car park where the Peugeot Partner had been left. They went down the street towards the police cordon where a group of people had gathered, waiting to be able to get back into their apartments.

'How was Fernando by the time you left him?' asked Falcón. 'I didn't catch his surname.'

'Fernando Alanis,' she said. 'He was more or less under control, considering what had happened to him. We've exchanged numbers.'

'Has he got anybody he can go to?'

'Not in Seville,' she said. 'His parents are up north and too old and sick. His sister lives in Argentina. His wife's family didn't approve of the marriage.'

'Friends?'

'His life was his family,' she said.

'Does he know what he's going to do?'

'I've told him he can come and stay with me.'

'You didn't have to do *that*, Cristina. He's not your responsibility.'

'You knew I'd offer though, didn't you, Inspector Jefe?' she said. 'If the situation demanded it.'

'I was going to put him up at my place,' said Falcón. 'You've got to go to work, the kids . . . you don't have any room.'

'He needs a sense of what he's lost,' she said. 'And who'd look after him at your place?'

'My housekeeper,' said Falcón. 'You won't believe me, but I really did not intend for that to happen.'

'We have to pull together or we let them win by falling apart,' she said. 'And you always choose me for this type of work – once a nun always a nun.'

'I don't remember saying that.'

'But you remember thinking it, and didn't you say that we weren't just foot soldiers in the fight against crime,' said Ferrera, 'but that we're here to help as well. We're the crusading detectives of Andalucía.'

'José Luis would laugh in your face if he heard you say that,' said Falcón. 'And you should be very wary of using words like that in *this* investigation.'

'Fernando was already accusing "the Moroccans",' she said. 'Ever since March 11th they've been watching them go into that mosque and wondering.'

'That's the way people's minds naturally work these days, and they like to have their suspicions confirmed,' said Falcón. 'We can't take their prejudices into this investigation. We have to examine the facts and keep them divorced from any natural assumptions. If we don't, we'll make the sort of mistakes they made right from the beginning in the Madrid bombings when they blamed ETA. Already there are confusing aspects to the evidence that we've found in the Peugeot Partner.'

'Explosives, copies of the Koran and a green sash and black hood don't sound confusing to me,' said Ferrera.

'Why two copies of the Koran? One brand-new

cheap Spanish edition and the other heavily used and annotated, but exactly the same edition.'

'The extra copy was a gift?'

'Why leave it in full view on the front seat? This is Seville, people usually leave their cars completely empty,' said Falcón. 'We need more information on these books. I want you to find out where they were bought and if there was a credit card or cheque used.'

He tore the page from his notebook with the ISBNs and bar codes, recopied them and gave Ferrera the torn page.

'What are we trying to find out from the occupants of this apartment block?'

'Keep it simple. Everybody's in shock. If we can find witnesses we'll bring them to this car park, ask whether they saw the Peugeot Partner arrive, if they saw anybody getting out of it, how many, what age and if they took anything out of the back.'

At the police cordon Falcón called out the address of the apartment block. An old man in his seventies came forward and a woman in her forties with a bruised face and a plastered arm in a sling. Falcón took the old man, Ferrera the woman. As they passed the entrance to their block a bomb squad man and a fireman confirmed that the building was now clear. Falcón showed the old man the Peugeot Partner and took him back up to his third-floor apartment, where the living room and kitchen were covered in glass, all the blinds in shreds, the chairs fallen over, photographs on the floor and the soft furniture lacerated, with brown foam already protruding from the holes.

The old man had been lying on his bed in the back of the apartment. His son and daughter-in-law had already left for work, with the kids, who were too old for the pre-school, so nobody had been hurt. He stood in the midst of his wrecked home with his left hand shaking and his old, rheumy eyes taking it all in.

'So you're here on your own all day,' said Falcón.

'My wife died last November,' he said.

'What do you do with yourself?'

'I do what old guys do: read the paper, take a coffee, look at the kids playing in the pre-school. I wander about, talk to people and choose the best time to smoke the three cigarettes I allow myself every day.'

Falcón went to the window and pulled the ruined blinds away.

'Do you remember seeing that van?'

'The world is full of small white vans these days,' said the old man. 'So I can't be sure whether I saw the same van twice, or different vans in two separate instances. On the way to the pharmacy I saw the van for the first time, driving from left to right down Calle Los Romeros, with two people in the front. It pulled into the kerb by the mosque and that was it.'

'What time?'

'About ten thirty yesterday morning.'

'And the next time?'

'About fifteen minutes later on the way back from the pharmacy I saw a white van pull into the parking area, but not in that spot. It was on the other side, facing away from us, and only one guy got out.'

'Did you see him clearly?'

'He was dark. I'd have said he was Moroccan. There are a lot of them around here. He had a round head, close-cropped hair, prominent ears.'

'Age?'

'About thirty. He looked fit. He had a tight black T-shirt on and he was muscled. I think he was wearing jeans and trainers. He locked the car and went off through the trees to Calle Blanca Paloma.'

'Did you see the van when it arrived in the position it is now?'

'No. All I can tell you is that it was there by six thirty in the evening. My daughter-in-law parked next to it. I also remember that when I went for coffee after lunch the van had left its position on the other side. There aren't so many cars during the day, except for the ones belonging to teachers lined up in front of the school, so I don't know how, but I noticed it. Old guys notice different things to other people.'

'And there were two men when it was going along Calle Los Romeros?'

'That's why I can't be sure if it was the same van.'

'On which side of the van did your daughter-in-law park her car?'

'To the left as we're looking at it,' said the old man. 'Her door was blown open by the wind and knocked into it.'

'Did the van move again at all?'

'No idea. Once people are around me I don't notice a thing.'

Falcón took the daughter-in-law's name and number and called her as he walked upstairs. He talked her through the conversation he'd just had with her father-in-law and asked her if she'd had a look at the van when her door had knocked into it.

'I checked it, just to make sure I hadn't dented it.'

'Did you glance in the window?'

113

'Probably.'

'Did you see anything on the front passenger seat?'

'No, nothing.'

'You didn't see a book?'

'Definitely not. It was just a dark seat.'

Ferrera was coming out of the fourth-floor apartment as he hung up. They went downstairs in silence.

'Was your witness injured in the blast?' asked Falcón.

'She *says* she fell down the stairs last night, but she's got no bruises on her arms or legs, just the ones on her face,' said Ferrera angrily. 'And she was scared.'

'Not of you.'

'Yes, of me. Because I ask questions, and one question leads to another, and if any of it somehow gets back to her husband it's another reason for him to beat her.'

'You can only help the ones that want to be helped,' said Falcón.

'There seems to be more of it about these days,' said Ferrera, exasperated. 'Anyway, she did see the van arrive in its current position. There's a woman on the same shift at the factory where she works, who lives in one of the blocks further down her street. They meet for a chat under the trees on Calle Blanca Paloma. They walked past the van at 6 p.m. just as it had arrived. Two guys got out. They were talking in Arabic. They didn't take anything out of the back. They went up to Calle Los Romeros and turned right.'

'Descriptions?'

'Both late twenties. One with a shaved head, black T-shirt. The other with more of a square head, with black hair, cut short at the sides and combed back on top. She said he was very good looking, but had bad teeth. He wore a faded denim jacket, white T-shirt, and she remembers he had very flashy trainers.'

'Did she see the van move again from that position?'

'She keeps an eye on this car park, looking out for when her husband comes home. She said it hadn't moved by the time he came in at 9.15 p.m.'

The police were letting people through the cordon so that they could get back into their homes to start clearing up the damage. There was a large crowd gathered outside the chemist's at the junction of Calle Blanca Paloma with Calle Los Romeros. They were angry with the police for not letting them back into any part of the block attached to the destroyed building, which was still too dangerous. Falcón tried talking to people in the crowd, but they couldn't give a damn about Peugeot Partners.

Pneumatic drills started up on the other side of the block. Falcón and Ferrera crossed Calle Los Romeros to another apartment building, whose glass was more or less intact. The apartments on the first two floors were still empty. On the third floor a child led Falcón into a living room, where a woman was sweeping up glass around a pile of cardboard boxes. She had moved in at the weekend but the removal company hadn't been able to deliver until yesterday. He asked his question about the white van and the two guys.

'Do you think I'd be sitting on the balcony watching the traffic with all this lot to unpack?' she said. 'I've had to give up two days' work because these people can't deliver on time.'

'Do you know who was in here before you?'

'It was empty,' she said. 'Nobody had been living

115

here for three months. The letting agency on Avenida San Lazaro said we were the first to see it.'

'Was there anything left here when you first arrived?' asked Falcón, looking out of the living-room balcony on to Calle Los Romeros and the rubble of the destroyed building.

'There was no furniture, if that's what you mean,' she said. 'There was a sack of rubbish in the kitchen.'

'What sort of rubbish?'

'People have been killed. *Children* have been killed,' she said, aghast, pulling her own child to her side. 'And you're asking me what sort of *rubbish* I found here when I moved in?'

'Police work can seem like a mysterious business,' said Falcón. 'If you can remember noticing anything it might help.'

'As it happens, I had to tie the bag up and throw it out, so I know that it was a pizza carton, a couple of beer cans, some cigarette butts, ash and empty packets and a newspaper, the *ABC*, I think. Anything else?'

'That's very good, because now we know that, although this place was empty for three months, somebody had been here, spending quite some time in this apartment, and that could be interesting for us.'

He crossed the landing to the apartment opposite. A woman in her sixties lived there.

'Your new neighbour has just told me that her apartment had been empty for the last three months,' he said.

'Not quite empty,' she said. 'When the previous family moved out, about four months ago, some very smart businessmen came round, on maybe three or four occasions. Then, about three months ago, a small

116

van turned up and unloaded a bed, two chairs and a table. Nothing else. After that, young men would turn up in pairs, and spend three or four hours at a time during the day, doing God knows what. They never spent the night there, but from dawn until dusk there was always someone in that apartment.'

'Did the same guys come back again, or were they different every time?'

'I think there might have been as many as twenty.'

'Did they bring anything with them?'

'Briefcases, newspapers, groceries.'

'Did you ever talk to them?'

'Of course. I asked them what they were doing and they just said that they were having meetings,' she said. 'I wasn't that worried. They didn't look like druggies. They didn't play loud music or have parties; in fact, quite the opposite.'

'Did their routine change over the months?'

'Nobody came during Semana Santa and the Feria.'

'Did you ever see inside the apartment when they were there?'

'In the beginning I offered them something to eat, but they always very politely refused. They never let me inside.'

'And they never let on about what these meetings were about?'

'They were such straight, conservative young men, I thought they might be a religious group.'

'What happened when they left?'

'One day a van arrived and took away the furniture and that was it.'

'When was that?'

'Last Friday . . . the second of June.'

117

Falcón called Ferrera and told her to keep at it while he went to talk to the letting agency down the street on Avenida de San Lazaro.

The woman in the letting agency had been responsible for selling the property three months ago and renting it out at the end of last week. It had not been bought by a private buyer but a computer company called Informáticalidad. All her dealings were through the Financial Director, Pedro Plata.

Falcón took down the address. Ramírez called him as he was walking back up Calle Los Romeros towards the bombed building.

'Comisario Elvira has just told me that the Madrid police have picked up Mohammed Soumaya at his shop. He lent the van to his nephew. He was surprised to hear that it was in Seville. His nephew had told him he was just going to use it for some local deliveries,' said Ramírez. 'They're following up on the nephew now. His name is Trabelsi Amar.'

'Are they sending us shots of him?'

'We've asked for them,' said Ramírez. 'By the way, they've just installed an Arabic speaker in the Jefatura, after receiving more than a dozen calls from our friends across the water. They all say the same thing and the translation is: "We will not rest until Andalucía is back in the bosom of Islam."'

'Have you ever heard of a company called Informáticalidad?' asked Falcón.

'Never,' said Ramírez, totally uninterested. 'There's one last bit of news for you. They've identified the explosive found in the back of the Peugeot Partner. It's called cyclotrimethylenetrinitramine.'

'And what's that?'

'Otherwise known as RDX. Research and Development Explosive,' said Ramírez, in a wobbly English accent. 'Its other names are cyclonite and hexogen. It's top-quality military explosive – the sort of thing you'd find in artillery shells.'

9

Ferrera had found one occupant who'd given her a sighting of the Peugeot Partner late yesterday afternoon, Monday 5th June. The van had stopped on Calle Los Romeros, opposite the mosque, and two men had unloaded four cardboard boxes and some blue plastic carrier bags. The only description of the men was that they were young and well built and were wearing T-shirts and jeans. The boxes were heavy enough that they could only be carried one at a time. Everything was taken into the mosque. Both men came out and drove away in the van. Falcón told her to keep looking for witnesses and if necessary to go down to the hospital.

Back in the car park the Mayor and the deputies from the Andalucían Parliament had gone and Comisario Elvira and Juez Calderón were coming to the end of an impromptu press conference. Another body had been found on the seventh floor. The rescue workers had not made contact with anybody alive in the rubble. Pneumatic drills were being used to expose the steel netting in the reinforced concrete floors and oxyacety-lene torches and motorized cutters were breaking up

120

the floors into slabs. These slabs were being lifted away by the crane and put into tippers. With each piece of information given, more questions came at them. Elvira was visibly irritated by it all, but Calderón was playing at the top of his game and the journalists loved him. They were more than happy to concentrate on the good-looking, charismatic Calderón when finally Elvira took his leave and headed into the pre-school, where they'd set up a temporary headquarters in the undamaged class-rooms at the back.

The journalists recognized Falcón and came after him, preventing him from following Elvira. Microphones butted his face. Cameras were thrust between heads. What's the name of the explosive again? Where did it come from? Are the terrorists still alive? Is there a cell still operating in Seville? What have you got to say about the evacuations in the city centre? Has there been another bomb? Has anybody claimed responsibility for the attack? Falcón had to force his way out of the scrum and it took three policemen to push the journalists back from the pre-school entrance. Falcón was straightening himself up in the corridor when Calderón burst through the roaring crowd at the gates.

'*Joder*,' he said, remaking his tie, 'they're like a pack of jackals.'

'Ramírez just told me about the explosive.'

'They keep asking me about that. I haven't heard anything.'

'The common name is RDX or hexogen.'

'Hexogen?' said Calderón. 'Wasn't that what the Chechen rebels used to blow up those apartment blocks in Moscow back in 1999?'

'The military use it in artillery shells.'

'I remember there was some scandal about the Chechens using recycled explosives from a government scientific research institute, which had been bought by the mafia, who then sold it to the rebels. Russian military ordnance being used to blow up their own people.'

'Sounds like a typical Russian scenario.'

'It's not going to be easy for you,' said Calderón. 'Hexogen can come from anywhere – Russia, a Muslim Chechen terrorist group, an arms dump in Iraq, any Third World country where there's been a conflict, where ordnance has been left behind. It might even be American, this stuff.'

Falcón's mobile vibrated. It was Elvira, calling them into a meeting with the Centro Nacional de Inteligencia and the antiterrorist squad of the Comisaría General de Información.

There were three men from the CNI. The boss was a man in his sixties, with white hair and dark eyebrows and a handsome, ex-athlete's face. He introduced himself only as Juan. His two juniors, Pablo and Gregorio, were younger men, who had the bland appearance of middle managers. In their dark suits they were barely distinguishable, although Pablo had a scar running from his hairline to his left eyebrow. Falcón was uncomfortably aware that Pablo had not taken his eyes off him since he'd walked into the room. He began to wonder whether they'd met before.

There was only one representative from the antiterrorism unit of the CGI. His name was Inspector Jefe Ramón Barros, a short, powerfully built man, with close-cropped grey hair and perfect teeth, which added a sinister element to his brutal and furious demeanour.

Comisario Elvira asked Falcón to give a résumé of

his findings so far. He started with the immediate after-math of the bomb and moved on quickly to the discovery of the Peugeot Partner, its contents, and the times it was seen by witnesses in the car park.

'We've since discovered that the fine white powder taken from the rear of the van is a military explosive known as hexogen, which my colleague, Juez Calderón, has told me was the same type of explosive used by Chechen rebels to blow up two apartment blocks in Moscow in 1999.'

'You can't believe everything you read in the news-papers,' said Juan. 'There's considerable doubt now that it was the Chechen rebels. We're not great believers in conspiracy theories in our own back yard, but when it comes to Russia it seems that anything is possible. There is a natural inclination, after such a catastrophic attack as this, to make comparisons to other terrorist attacks, to look for patterns. What we've learnt from the mistakes we made after March 11th is that there *are* no patterns. It's the government's business to quell panic by offering some kind of order to a terrified public. It's our job to treat every situation as unique. Carry on, Inspector Jefe.'

None of the Sevillanos liked this patronizing little speech and they looked at the CNI man in his expen-sive loafers, lightweight suit and stiff, heavy, silvery tie and decided that the only thing he'd said that didn't mark him out as a typical visiting Madrileño was his admission of a mistake.

'If it wasn't Chechen rebels, who was it?' asked Calderón.

'Not relevant, Juez Calderón,' said Juan. 'Proceed, Inspector Jefe.'

'It might be interesting from the point of view of sources for the hexogen,' said Calderón, who was not a man to be brushed off easily. 'We've found a van with traces of explosive and Islamic paraphernalia. The Chechens are known to have access to Russian military ordnance and have the sympathy of the Muslim world. In most people's minds those rebels were responsible for the destruction of the Moscow apartment blocks. If any of these connections have been proven invalid by the intelligence community, then perhaps the Inspector Jefe should know about them now. The source of the explosives will be an important area of his investigation.'

'*His* investigation?' said Juan. '*Our* investigation. This is going to be a concerted effort. The Grupo de Homicidios is not going to crack this case on its own. This hexogen will have been imported. The CNI has the international connections to find out where it came from.'

'Nevertheless,' said Calderón, embarking on some of his own pomposity, 'this is where the investigation begins, and if the Inspector Jefe is about to pursue an avenue of enquiry with incorrect or misleading information, then perhaps he should be told.'

Calderón was aware that this *was* irrelevant in terms of information for the purposes of the investigation, but he also knew that a demonstration of power was required to put Juan in his place. Calderón was the leading Juez de Instrucción and he was not going to have his authority undermined by an outsider, especially a Madrileño.

'We cannot be certain,' said Juan, exasperated by the posturing, 'but a theory is being given credibility that the Russian Security Service, the FSB, were *themselves* responsible for the outrage, and that they successfully managed to frame the Chechens. Just prior to the explosion Putin had become director of the FSB. The country was in turmoil and there was the perfect opportunity for a power play. The FSB provoked a war in Chechnya and Dagestan. The prime minister lost his job and Putin took over at the beginning of 1999. The Moscow apartment explosions gave him the opportunity to start a patriotic campaign. He was the fearless leader who would stand up to the rebels. By the beginning of 2000, Putin was acting president of Russia. The hexogen used by the FSB was supposed to have come from a scientific research institute in Lubyanka where the FSB has its headquarters. As you can see, Juez Calderón, my explanation does not help us very much here, but it does illustrate how very quickly the world can become a dangerous and confusing place.'

Silence, while the Sevillanos considered the reverberations of the explosion in their own city to places like Chechnya and Moscow. Falcón continued his briefing about the Peugeot Partner, the two men seen unloading goods for the mosque, the men believed to have been in the mosque at the time of the explosion, and the latest revelations about the owner of the vehicle and his nephew, Trabelsi Amar, who had borrowed it.

'Anything else?' asked Juan, while Elvira's assistant entered the name of Trabelsi Amar into the terrorist suspects database.

'Just one thing to clear up before I continue with the investigation,' said Falcón. 'Did the CNI or the CGI have the mosque under surveillance?'

'What makes you think that we might have done?' asked Juan.

Falcón briefed them on the mysterious, well-dressed young men from Informáticalidad, who had frequented the nearby apartment over the past three months.

'That is not the way *we* would run a surveillance operation and I've never heard of Informáticalidad.'

'What about the antiterrorism unit, Inspector Jefe Barros?' asked Elvira.

'We did not have the mosque under active surveillance,' said Barros, who seemed to be restraining great anger under preternatural calm. 'I've heard of Informáticalidad. They're the biggest suppliers of computer software and consumables in Seville. They even supply us.'

'One final question about the Imam,' said Falcón. 'We're told he arrived here from Tunis in September 2004 and that he is in the lowest risk category for terrorist suspects, but his history required a higher authority for clearance.'

'His file is incomplete,' said Juan.

'What does that mean?'

'As far as we know, he's clean,' said Juan. 'He has been heard to speak out against the cold-blooded, indiscriminate nature of the Madrid bombings. We understand from his visa application that part of the reason he came to Seville was to attempt a healing of the wounds between the Catholic and Muslim communities. He saw that as his duty. We were only concerned about gaps in his history that we could not fill. These gaps occurred in the 1980s, when a lot of Muslims went to Afghanistan to fight with the mujahedeen against the Russians. Some returned radicalized to their homes in the 1990s and others later became the Taliban. The Imam would have been in his thirties at the time and therefore a prime candidate. In the end, the Americans vouched for him and we allowed him a visa.'

'So this bomb has killed a potential sympathizer, five men over the age of sixty-five, a man under thirty-five who was in a wheelchair, two Spanish converts and two men in their forties collecting disability benefits, which leaves only two under the age of thirty-five, able-bodied and of North African origin,' said Elvira. 'Can the CNI offer a theory as to why this strangely mixed group of people who, we have just been told, were not under active surveillance, should be storing high-quality military explosive and why it should have been detonated?'

Silence. The grinding gears of the machinery outside reached them. The thunder of rubble dropping into empty tippers, the hiss and scream of hydraulics, the low roar of the crane's unwinding cable, all punctuated by the pneumatic drills' staccato stabbing, reminded these men of the purpose of their meeting and the disaster that had befallen this city.

'Trabelsi Amar is not on any terrorist suspect database and he's an illegal alien,' said Elvira's assistant, breaking the silence.

'Do you believe that explosives could have been stored in the mosque without the knowledge of the Imam?' asked Calderón.

'There's an outside chance that he didn't recognize what it was,' said Juan. 'As you know, hexogen looks like sugar. The trace left on the floor indicates that the packaging wasn't exactly hermetically sealed. It's possible that the explosive was in those cardboard boxes, which the Inspector Jefe has told us were seen being unloaded yesterday.'

'But for the hexogen to actually explode would require a detonator,' said Falcón. 'From the way in which they were moving it around it must be a stable product.'

'It is,' said Juan.

'Then that means they must have been working on making bombs and accidentally detonated it,' said Falcón. 'I doubt they could be doing that in secret in a mosque of that size, with thirteen other people in it. I haven't seen the plans, but it can't be more than ten by twenty metres.'

'So the Imam is complicit in that scenario,' said Juan. 'We'll have to talk to the Americans about Abdelkrim Benaboura and we'll find a photo ID and a history for Trabelsi Amar.'

'If Soumaya is identifying Amar as his nephew, then that doesn't sound to me like deep terrorist cover. He's probably got photographs,' said Falcón. 'We have to consider the possibility that this van was not being driven by him. It could have been stolen or, for whatever reason, given to another party to transport goods to Seville. Trabelsi Amar's function could have been simply to provide a van, which would not be reported stolen.'

'We'll make sure the CGI in Canillas communicate with the local police in Madrid, who are interviewing Mohammed Soumaya,' said Juan, which sounded like he was undermining Inspector Jefe Barros, who was still boiling in silence. 'It's one of the complications of these terrorist operations that the people we know about are active only in so far as they use up our time and resources. As was the case with March 11th, where none of the operatives were known terrorists or had any links to known radical Islamic organizations. They came out of nowhere to perform their tasks.'

'But you're in a better position now than you were then,' said Elvira.

'Since 9/11 and the evidence of connections made by Islamic terrorist cell members in Spain . . .'

'You mean al-Qaeda members?' said Elvira.

'We don't like to use the name al-Qaeda because it implies an organization with a hierarchy along Western lines. This is not the case,' said Juan. 'It's useful for the media to have this name to hang on Islamic terrorism, but we don't use it in the service. We have to remind ourselves not to be complacent. As I was saying: since 9/11 and the evidence of connections made by Islamic terrorist cell members in Spain with the perpetrators of the Twin Towers and Washington DC attacks, there has been considerable stepping up of activities.'

'But, as you say, there seems to be an unending stream of young operatives who you don't know about and who can be organized at a distance to perform terrorist acts,' said Calderón. 'That, surely, is the problem?'

'As you've seen from the investigations into the London bombings, there is extraordinary co-operation between all the secret services,' said Juan. 'Our proximity to North Africa makes us vulnerable but gives us opportunities as well. In the two years since the Madrid train bombings we have achieved considerable penetration into Morocco, Algeria and Tunisia. We hope to improve our ability to pick up sleeping cells by intercepting the signals that might eventually activate them. We are not perfect, but neither are they. You don't hear about our successes, and it's too early to say whether we are dealing here with one of our failures.'

'You said that "in this scenario the Imam is complicit",' said Falcón. 'Does this mean you are looking at other scenarios?'

'All we can do is prepare ourselves for eventualities,' said Juan. 'In the last two years we have been examining a domestic phenomenon, which first came to light on the internet. I hesitate to call this phenomenon a group, because we have found no evidence of organization, or communication, for that matter. What we have found are newsletter pages on a website called www.vomit.org. This was thought to be an American site because it first appeared in the English language, but the CIA and MI5 have just recently told us they now believe VOMIT stands for Victimas del Odio de Musulmanos, Islamistas y Terroristas.'

'What's the content of the newsletter?'

'It's an updated list of all terrorist attacks carried out by Islamic extremists since the early 1990s. It gives a short account of the attack, the number of victims, both dead and injured, followed by the number of people directly affected by the death or injury of a person close to them.'

'Does that mean they are contacting the victims' families?' asked Elvira.

'If they are, the victims seem to be unaware of it,' said Juan. 'Victims get approached by the media, the government, the social services, the police . . . and, as yet, we haven't found anyone who has been able to tell us that they've been contacted by VOMIT.'

'Did this start in 2004 after the Madrid bombings?' said Elvira.

'The British first came across the pages in June 2004. By September 2004 it also included Muslim on Muslim attacks, such as suicide bombings against police recruiting offices in Iraq, and since the beginning of 2005 there has also been a section on Muslim women who have been the victims of honour killings or gang rapes. In these cases, they only report on the type of attack and number of victims.'

'Presumably the posting of these pages on the web is completely anonymous,' said Calderón, who didn't wait for an answer. 'There must have been a Muslim reaction to this, surely?'

'The Al Jazeera news channel did a piece on these web pages back in August 2004 and there was a huge internet response in which various Arab-sponsored websites enumerated Arab victims of Israeli, American, European, Russian, Far Eastern and Australian aggression. Some of them were extreme and went back in history to the Crusades, the expulsion of the Moors from Spain and the defeat of the Ottoman empire. None of the websites came up with as powerful a banner as VOMIT, and a lot of them couldn't resist spouting an agenda, so although they were read avidly in the Arab world, they didn't penetrate the West at all.'

'So what makes you think that VOMIT has gone from being a passive, unorganized internet phenomenon into an active, operational entity?' asked Falcón.

'We don't,' said Juan. 'We review their web pages daily to see if there's any incitement to violence, disrespect shown to Islam, or attempts at recruitment to some kind of cause, but there's nothing except the clocking up of attacks and their victims.'

'Have you spoken to victims of the Madrid bombings?' asked Falcón.

'There is no common theme of vengeance amongst them. The only anger was directed at our own politicians and not against North Africans in general, or Islamic fanatics specifically. Most of the victims recognized that many Muslims had also been killed in the bombings. They saw it as an indiscriminate act of terror, with a political goal.'

'Did any of them know about VOMIT?'

'Yes, but none of them said they would seek membership if it existed,' said Juan. 'However, we do know that there is anger out there from fanatical right-wing groups with strong racist views and anti-immigration policies. We are keeping an eye on them. The police handle their violent activities at a local level. They are not known to have a national organization or to have planned and carried out attacks of this magnitude.'

'And religious groups?'

'Some of these fanatically right-wing groups have religious elements, too. If they advertise themselves in any way, we know about them. What concerns us is that they might be learning from their perceived enemies.'

'So the other possible scenario – that this was an organized attack against a Muslim community – is based solely on what? That it's about time there was a reaction against Islamic terrorism?' asked Calderón.

'Each terrorist atrocity is unique. The circumstances that prevail at the time make it so,' said Juan. 'At the time of the March 11th attack, Aznar's government were *expecting* an ETA attempt to disrupt the forthcoming elections. A couple of months earlier on

Christmas Eve 2003 two bombs of 25 kilos each had been discovered on the Irún–Madrid intercity train. Both bombs were classic ETA devices and had been set to explode two minutes before their arrival in the Chamartín station. Another ETA bomb was found on the track of the Zaragoza–Caspe–Barcelona line, which was set to explode on New Year's Eve 2003. On 29th February 2004, as everybody in this room knows, the Guardia Civil intercepted two ETA operatives in a transit van which contained 536 kilos of Titadine, destination Madrid. Everything was pointing to a major attack on the railway system prior to the elections on 14th March 2004, which would be planned and carried out by ETA.'

'That was the information, and the extrapolation from it was sent to the government by the CNI,' said Calderón, keen to stick it in.

'And it was wrong, Juez Calderón. *We* were wrong,' said Juan. 'Even after listening to the tapes of the Koran found in the Renault Kangoo van near the Alcalá de Henares station, and the discovery of the detonators not previously used by ETA, and the fact that the explosive was not Titadine, as customarily used by ETA, but Goma 2 ECO, we still couldn't believe that ETA was *not* behind it. *That* is the very point I am making, and it is why we should consider all scenarios in this present attack and not allow our minds to harden around a core of received opinion. We must work, step by step, until we have the unbreakable line of logic that leads to the perpetrators.'

'We can't leave people in the dark while we do this,' said Calderón. 'The media, the politicians and the public need to know that something is happening, that their safety is assured. Terror breeds confusion –'

'Comisario Elvira, as leader of this investigation, has that responsibility, as do the politicians. Our job is to make sure that they have the right information,' said Juan. 'We've already started looking at this attack with a historical mind – the apartment bombs in Moscow, the discovery of Islamic paraphernalia in a white van – and we can't afford to do that.'

'The media already knows what was found in the Peugeot Partner van,' said Calderón. 'We cannot prevent them from drawing their conclusions.'

'*How* do they know that?' asked Juan. 'There was a police cordon.'

'We don't know,' said Calderón, 'but as soon as the vehicle was removed and the journalists allowed into the car park, Comisario Elvira and I were fielding questions about the hexogen, the two copies of the Koran, a hood, the Islamic sash, and plenty of other stuff that wasn't even in the van.'

'There were a lot of people out in that car park,' said Falcón. 'My officers, the forensics, the bomb squad, the vehicle removal men, were all in the vicinity of that first inspection of the van. Journalists do their job. The cameras were supposed to be kept away from the bodies of the children in the pre-school, but one guy found his way in there.'

'As we've seen before,' said Juan, breathing down his irritation, 'it's very difficult to dislodge first impressions from the public's mind. There are still millions of Americans who believe that Saddam Hussein was responsible in some way for 9/11. Most of Seville will now believe that they have been the victim of an Islamic terrorist attack and we might not be able to come close to confirming the truth of the matter until we can get into the mosque, which could be days of demolition work away.'

'Perhaps we should look at the unique circumstances which led to this event,' said Falcón, 'and also look at the future, to see if there's anything that this bombing might be seeking to influence. From my own point of view, the reason I was very early on to the scene here was that I was at the Forensic Institute, discussing the autopsy of a body found on the main rubbish dump on the outskirts of Seville.'

Falcón gave the details of the unidentifiable corpse found yesterday.

'This could, of course, be an unconnected murder,' said Falcón. 'However, it is unique in the crime history of Seville and it does not appear to be the work of a single person, but rather a group of killers, who have gone to extreme lengths to prevent identification.'

'Have there been any other murders with similar attempts to prevent identification?' asked Juan.

'Not in Spain this year, according to the police computer,' said Falcón. 'We haven't checked with Interpol yet. Our investigation is still very new.'

'Are there any elections due?'

'The Andalucían parliamentary elections last took place in March 2004,' said Calderón. 'The Town Hall elections were in 2003 so they are due next March. The socialists are currently in office.'

Juan took a folded piece of paper out of his pocket.

'Before we left Madrid we had a call from the CGI, who had just been informed by the editor of the *ABC* that they had received a letter with a Seville stamp on the envelope. The letter consisted of a single sheet of paper and a printed text in Spanish. We have since discovered that this text comes from the work of Abdullah Azzam, a preacher best known as the leading ideologue of the Afghan resistance to the Russian invasion. It reads as follows:

'"This duty will not end with victory in Afghanistan; jihad will remain an individual obligation until all other lands that were Muslim are returned to us, so that Islam will reign again: before us lie Palestine, Bokhara, Lebanon, Chad, Eritrea, Somalia, the Philippines, Burma, Southern Yemen, Tashkent . . ."' he paused, looking around the room, '"and Andalucía."'

10

The meeting broke up with the news that another body had been found in the rubble. Calderón left immediately. The three CNI men spoke intently amongst themselves, while Falcón and Elvira discussed resources. Inspector Jefe Barros of the CGI stared into the floor, his jaw muscles working over some new humiliation. After ten minutes the CNI conferred with Elvira. Falcón and Barros were asked to leave the room. Barros paced the corridor, avoiding Falcón. Some moments later Elvira called Falcón back in and the CNI men moved towards the door, saying that they would conduct a detailed search of Imam Abdelkrim Benaboura's apartment.

'Is that information going to be shared?' asked Falcón.

'Of course,' said Juan, 'unless it compromises national security.'

'I'd like one of my officers to be present.'

'In the light of what's just been said, we have to do it now and you're all too busy.'

They left. Falcón turned to Elvira, hands open, questioning this state of affairs.

'They're determined not to make a mistake this time round,' said Elvira, '*and* they want all the credit for it, too. Futures are at stake here.'

'And to what extent do you have control over what they do?'

'Those words "national security" are the problem,' said Elvira. 'For instance, they want to talk to *you* on a matter of "national security", which means I'm told nothing other than it has to be private and at length.'

'That's not going to be easy today.'

'They'll make time for you – at night, whenever.'

'And "national security" is the only clue they've given?'

'They're interested in your Moroccan connections,' said Elvira, 'and have asked to interview you.'

'Interview me?' said Falcón. 'That sounds like it's for a job and I've already got one of those with plenty of work in it.'

'Where are you going now?'

'I'm tempted to be present at the search of the Imam's apartment,' said Falcón. 'But I think I'm going to follow up the Informáticalidad lead. That's a very strange way to use an apartment for three months.'

'So you're keeping an open mind on this, unlike our CNI friends,' said Elvira, nodding at the door.

'I thought Juan was very eloquent on the subject.'

'That's how they want everybody else to think, so that they've got all their bases covered,' said Elvira, 'but there's no doubt in my mind that they believe they've hit on the beginning of a major Islamic terrorist campaign.'

'To bring Andalucía back into the Islamic fold?'

'Why else would they want to talk to you about your "Moroccan connections"?'

'We don't know what *they* know.'

'I know that they're seeking redress and greater glory,' said Elvira, 'and that worries me.'

'And what was going on with Inspector Jefe Barros?' asked Falcón. 'He was present but nothing more, as if he'd been told he was allowed to attend but not to say a word.'

'There's a problem, which they will explain to you directly. All I have been told by the head of the CGI in Madrid is that, for the moment, the Seville antiterrorism unit cannot contribute to this investigation.'

Consuelo sat in her office in the restaurant in La Macarena. She had kicked off her shoes and was curled up foetally on her new expensive leather office chair, which rocked her gently backwards and forwards. She had a ball of tissue in her hands, which was crammed into her mouth. She bit against it when the physical pain became too much. Her throat tried to articulate the emotion, but it had no reference points. Her body felt like ruptured earth, spewing up sharp chunks of magma.

The television was on. She had not been able to bear the silence of the restaurant. The chefs weren't due to start preparing the lunch service until 11 a.m. She had tried to walk her extreme agitation out of herself, but her tour of the spotless kitchen, with its gleaming stainless steel surfaces, its knives and cleavers winking encouragement at her, had terrified rather than calmed. She'd walked the dining rooms and the patio, but none of the smells, the textures, not even the obsessive order of the table settings could fill this aching emptiness pressing against her ribs.

She had retreated to her office, locked herself in. The volume of the television was turned low so that she couldn't make out the words, but she took comfort from the human murmur. She looked out of the corner of her eye at the images of destruction playing on the screen. There was the sharp smell of vomit in the room as she'd just thrown up at the sight of the tiny bodies under their pinafores outside the pre-school. Tears tracked mascara down her cheeks. The mouth side of the ball of tissue was slimy with sharp saliva. Something had been levered open; the lid was no longer on what-ever it was she had inside her, and she, who had always prided herself on her courage to face up to things, could not bear to take a look. She squeezed her eyes shut at a new rising of pain. The chair empathized with the shudder of her body. Her throat squealed as if there was something sharp lodged across it.

The destroyed apartment block flickered on the screen in the corner of her eye. She couldn't bear to switch off the TV and live with the only other occu-pant of the silence, even though the building's collapse was an appalling replication of her own mental state. Only a few hours ago she had been more or less whole. She had always imagined the gap between sanity and madness as a yawning chasm, but now found it was like a border in the desert: you didn't know whether you'd crossed it or not.

The TV pictures changed from the piles of rubble to a body bag being lifted into a cradle stretcher, to the wounded, staggering down pavements, to the jagged edges of shattered windows, to the trees stripped of all their leaves, to cars upside down in gardens, to a road sign speared into the earth. These TV news editors must be professionals in horror, every image was like a slap to the face, knocking a complacent public into the new reality.

Then calm returned. A presenter stood in front of the church of San Hermenegildo. He had a friendly face. Consuelo turned up the sound in the hope of good news. The camera zoomed in on the plaque and dropped back down to the presenter, who was now walking and giving a brief history of the church. The camera remained tight on the presenter's face. There was an inexplicable tension in the scene. Something was coming. The suspense transfixed Consuelo. The presenter's voice told them that this was the site of an old mosque and the camera cut to the apex of a classic Arabic arch. Its focus pulled wide to reveal the new horror. Written in red over the doors were the words: *AHORA ES NUESTRA*. Now it is ours.

The screen filled again with another montage of horror. Women screaming for no apparent reason. Blood on the pavements, in the gutter, thickening the dust. A body, with the terrible sag of lifelessness, being lifted out of the ruins.

She couldn't bear the sight of any more. These cameramen must be robots to handle this horror. She turned the TV off and sat in the silence of the office.

The images had jolted her. The lid seemed to have slipped back over the darkness welling inside her chest. Her hands trembled, but she no longer needed to bite on the ball of tissue. The shame of her first consultation with Alicia Aguado came back to her. Consuelo pressed her hands to her cheekbones as she remembered her words: 'blind bitch'. How could she have said such a thing? She picked up the phone.

141

Alicia Aguado was relieved to hear Consuelo's voice. Her concern raised emotion in Consuelo's throat. Nobody ever cared about her. She stumbled through an apology.

'I've been called worse than that,' said Aguado. 'Given that we're the most inventive insulters in the world, you can imagine the special reserves that are drawn on when it comes to psychologists.'

'It was unforgivable.'

'All will be forgiven as long as you come and see me again, Sra Jiménez.'

'Call me Consuelo. After what we've been through, all formality is out of the window,' she said. 'When can you see me?'

'I'd like to see you tonight, but it won't be possible before 9 p.m.'

'Tonight?'

'I'm very concerned about you. I wouldn't normally ask, but . . .'

'But what?'

'I think you've reached a very dangerous point.'

'Dangerous? Dangerous to whom?'

'You have to promise me something, Consuelo,' said Aguado. 'You have to come directly here to me after work, and when our consultation is over you must go straight home and have somebody – a relative or a friend – to be there with you.'

Silence from Consuelo.

'I could ask my sister, I suppose,' she said.

'It's very important,' said Aguado. 'I think you've realized the extreme vulnerability of your state, so I would recommend that you confine yourself to home, work and my consulting room.'

'Can you just explain that to me?'

'Not now over the phone, face to face this evening,' she said. 'Remember, come straight to me. You must resist all temptations to any diversion, however strong the urge.'

Manuela Falcón sat in Angel's big comfortable chair in front of the television. She was now incapable of movement, with not even the strength to reach for the remote and shut down the screen, which was transferring the horror images directly to her mind. The police were evacuating El Corte Inglés in the Plaza del Duque after four reports of suspicious packages on different floors of the department store. Two sniffer dogs and their handlers arrived to patrol the building. The image cut to a deserted crossroads in the heart of the city, with shoes scattered over the cobbles and people running towards the Plaza Nueva. Manuela felt pale, with just the minimum quantity of blood circulating around her head and face to maintain basic oxygenation and brain function. Her extremities were freezing, despite the open door to the terrace and the temperature outside steadily rising.

The telephone had rung once since Angel had left for the *ABC* offices where he hoped to put his finger to the thready pulse of a convulsing city. She'd had the strength then to answer it. Her lawyer had asked whether she'd seen the television and then told her that the Sevillana buyer had pulled out with an excuse about her 'black' money not being ready and that she would have to postpone the signing of the deed.

'That's not going to stop her from losing her deposit,' said Manuela, still able to raise some aggression.

143

'Have you been listening to what Canal Sur have been reporting?' said the lawyer. 'They've found a van with traces of a military explosive in the back. The editor of the *ABC* in Madrid was sent a letter from al-Qaeda saying that they would not rest until Andalucía was back in the Islamic fold. There's some security expert saying that this is the start of a major terrorist campaign and there'll be more attacks in the coming days.'

'Fucking hell,' said Manuela, jamming a cigarette into her mouth, lighting it.

'So that 20,000 deposit your buyer might lose is looking like a cheap way out for her.'

'What about the German's lawyer, has he called yet?'

'Not yet, but he's going to.'

Manuela had clicked off the phone and let it fall in her lap. She smoked on automatic with great fervour, and the nicotine surge enabled her to call Angel, whose mobile was off. They couldn't find him in the *ABC* offices, which sounded like the trading floor in the first minutes of a black day for the markets.

Her lawyer called again.

'The German has pulled out. I've called the notary's office and all deed signings have been cancelled for the day. There's been an announcement on the TV and radio, the Jefe Superior de la Policía and the chief of the emergency services have told us to only use mobile phones if absolutely necessary.'

The workshop was in a courtyard up an old alleyway with massive grey cobbles, off Calle Bustos Tavera. Marisa Moreno had rented it purely because of this alleyway. On bright sunny days, such as this one, the

144

light in the courtyard was so intense that nothing could be discerned from within the darkness of the twenty-five-metre alleyway. The cobbles were like pewter ingots and drew her on. Her attraction to this alleyway was that it coincided with her vision of death. Its arched interior was not pretty, with crappy walls, a collection of fuse boxes and electric cables running over crumbling whitewashed plaster. But that was the point. It was a transference from this messy, material world to the cleansing white light beyond. There was, however, disappointment in the courtyard, to find that paradise was a broken-down collection of shabby workshops and storage houses, with peeling paint, wrought-iron grilles and rusted axles.

It was only a five-minute walk from her apartment on Calle Hiniesta to her workshop, which was another reason she'd rented somewhere too big for her needs. She occupied the first floor, accessed via an iron staircase to the side. It had a huge window overlooking the courtyard, which gave light and great heat in the summer. Marisa liked to sweat; that was the Cuban in her. She often worked in bikini briefs and liked the way the wood chips from her carving stuck to her skin.

That morning she'd left her apartment and taken a coffee in one of the bars on Calle Vergara. The bar was unusually packed, with all heads turned to the television. She ordered her café con leche, drank it and left, refusing all attempts by the locals to involve her in any debate. She had no interest in politics, she didn't believe in the Catholic Church or any other organized religion, and, as far as she was concerned, terrorism only mattered if you happened to be in the wrong place at the wrong time.

In the studio she worked on staining two carvings and polishing another two, ready for delivery. By midday she had them rolled in bubblewrap and was down in the courtyard waiting for a taxi.

A young Mexican dealer, who had a gallery in the centre on Calle Zaragoza, had bought the two pieces. He was part Aztec, and Marisa had had an affair with him a few months before she'd met Esteban Calderón. He still bought every carving she made and paid cash on delivery every time. To see them greet each other you might have thought they were still seeing each other, but it was more of a blood understanding, his Aztec and her African.

Esteban Calderón knew nothing of this. He'd never seen her workshop. She didn't have any of her work in her apartment. He knew she carved wood, but she made it sound as if it was in the past. That was the way she wanted it. She hated listening to Westerners talking about art. They didn't seem to grasp that appreciation was the other way around: let the piece talk to you.

Marisa dropped off her two finished pieces and took her money. She went to a tobacconist and bought herself a Cuban cigar – a Churchill from the Romeo y Julieta brand. She walked past the Archivo de las Indias and the Alcázar. The tourists were not quite as numerous as usual, but still there, and seemingly oblivious to the bomb which had gone off on the other side of the city, proving her point that terrorism only mattered if it directly affected you.

She walked through the Barrio Santa Cruz and into

the Murillo Gardens to indulge in her after-sales ritual. She sat on a park bench, unscrewed the aluminium cap of the cylinder and let the cigar fall into her palm. She smoked it under the palm trees, imagining herself back in Havana.

Inés had pulled herself together after fifteen minutes weeping. Her stomach couldn't take it any more. The tensing of her abdominals was agony. She had crawled to the shower, pulled off her nightdress and slumped in the tray, keeping her burning scalp out from under the fine needles of water.

After another quarter of an hour she had been able to stand, although not straight because of the pain in her side. She dressed in a dark suit with a high-collared cream blouse and put on heavy make-up. There was no bruising to disguise but she needed a full mask to get through the morning. She found some aspirin, which took the edge off the pain so that she could walk without being creased over to one side. Normally she would walk to work, but that was out of the question this morning and she took a taxi. That was the first she knew of the bomb. The radio was full of it. The driver talked non-stop. She sat in the back, silent behind her dark glasses until the driver, unnerved by her lack of response, asked if she was ill. She told him she had a lot on her mind. That was enough. At least he knew she was hearing him. He went into a long soliloquy about terrorism, how the only cure for this disease was to get rid of the lot of them.

'Who?' asked Inés.

'Muslims, Africans, Arabs . . . the whole lot. Get shot

of them all. Spain should be for the Spanish,' he said. 'What we need now are the old Catholic kings. They understood the need to be pure. They knew what they had to do . . .'

'So you're including the Jews in this mass exile?' she asked.

'*No, no, no que no,* the Jews are all right. It's these Moroccans, Algerians and Tunisians. They're all fanatics. They can't control their religious fervour. What are they doing, blowing up an apartment block? What does that prove?'

'It proves how powerful indiscriminate terror can be,' she said, feeling her whole chest about to burst open. 'We're no longer safe in our own homes.'

The Palacio de Justícia was frantic as usual. She slowly went up to her office on the second floor, which she shared with two other fiscales, state prosecutors. She was determined not to show the pain each step unleashed in her side. Having wanted to wear the badge of his violence, she now wanted to disguise her agony.

The mask of her make-up got her through the first excited minutes with her colleagues, who were full of the latest rumour and theory, with hardly a fact between them. Nobody associated Inés with emotional wreckage so they glided over the surface and went back to their work unaware of her state.

There were cases to prepare and meetings to be attended and Inés got through it all until the early afternoon when she found herself with a spare half-hour. She decided to go for a walk in the Murillo Gardens, which were just across the avenue. The gardens would calm her down and she wouldn't have to listen to any more conjecture about the bomb. She had the little grenade attack in her relationship to consider. She knew a breather in the park wasn't going to help her sort it out, but at least she might be able to find something around which to start rebuilding her collapsed marriage.

Over the last four years when things had been going wrong for Inés in her marriage she played herself a film loop. It was the edited version of her life with Esteban. It never started with their meeting each other and the subsequent affair, because that would mean the film started with her infidelity, and she did not see herself as somebody who broke her marriage vows. In her movie she was unblemished. She had rewritten her private history and cut out all images that did not meet with her approval. This was not a conscious act. There was no facing up to unfortunate episodes or personal embarrassments, they were simply forgotten.

This movie would have been immensely dull to anyone who was not Inés. It was propaganda. No better than a dictator's glorious biopic. Inés was the courageous fiancée who had picked up her husband-to-be after the nasty little incident that they never talked about, given him the care and attention he needed to get his career back on track . . . and so it went on. And it worked. For her. After each of his discovered infidelities she'd played the movie and it had given her strength; or rather it had given her something to record over Esteban's previous aberration, so that she only suffered from one of his infidelities at a time, and not the whole history.

This time, as she sat on the park bench playing her

film, something went wrong. She couldn't hold the images. It was as if the film was jumping out of the sprockets and letting an alien image flood into her private theatre: someone with long coppery hair, dark skin and splayed legs. This visual interference was shorting out her internal comfort loop. Inés gathered the amnesiac forces of her considerable mind by pressing her hands to the sides of her head and blinkering her eyes. It was then that she realized that it was something on the outside, forcing its way in. Reality was intruding. The copper-haired, dark-skinned whore she'd seen only this morning, naked, on her husband's digital camera was sitting opposite her, smoking a cigar without a care in the world.

Marisa didn't like the way the woman sitting on the bench on the other side of the shaded pathway was looking at her. She had the intensity of a lunatic about her; not the raving-in-the-asylum type but a more dangerous version: too thin, too chic, too shallow. She'd come across them at the Mexican dealer's gallery openings, all on the verge of a nervous breakdown. They filled the air with high-pitched chatter to keep the real world from bursting through the levee, as if, by chanting their consumer mantras, the great nothing that was going on in their lives would be kept at bay. In the gallery she tolerated their presence as they might buy her work, but out in the open she was not going to have one of these *cabras ricas* ruining her expensive cigar.

'What you looking at?' said Marisa. 'You're ruining my cigar, you know that?'

It took a moment for Inés, fluttering her eyelids in

astonishment, to realize that this was directed at her. Then the adrenaline kicked into her prosecutorial system. Here was a confrontation. She was good at those.

'I'm looking at you. *La puta con el puro,*' said Inés. The whore with the cigar.

Marisa uncrossed her legs and leaned forward, with her elbows on her knees, to get a good look at her heavily made-up adversary. She didn't stop to think too long.

'Hey, look, you bony-assed bitch, I'm sorry if I'm on your patch, but I'm not working, I'm just enjoying a cigar.'

The insult slashed across Inés's face leaving it red with outrage. The blood dimmed Inés's vision at the edges and played havoc with her oral-cerebral linkage.

'I'm a fucking lawyer!' she roared, and the people in the park stopped to look.

'Lawyers are the biggest whores of them all,' said Marisa. 'Is that why you paint your face like that? To hide the pox?'

Inés leapt to her feet, forgetting her injuries. Even in her fury she felt that twinge in her side, the bumping of her bruised organs, and it was that which stopped her from a full physical onslaught. That, and the force field of Marisa's languid muscularity, and impassive vocal brutality.

'*You* are the whore,' she said, pointing a spindly white finger at Marisa's lustrous, mulatto sheen. 'You're the one fucking *my* husband.'

The shock that registered in Marisa's face encouraged Inés, who had misread it as consternation.

'How much is he paying you?' asked Inés. 'It doesn't

151

look as if it's much more than 15 Euros a night, and that's a disgrace. That's not even minimum wage. Or does he throw in the copper wig and buy you a fat cigar to keep you happy when he's not there?'

Marisa instantly recovered from the revelation that this was the pale, pathetic, stringy little wife that Esteban couldn't bear to go back to. She'd also seen that wince of pain as Inés had got to her feet and guessed at the hurt being disguised by the clownish panstick. She'd seen beaten women in the poverty of Havana and she could spot vulnerability at a hundred metres, *and* she had the ruthlessness to open it up and reveal it to its owner and the rest of the world.

'Just remember, Inés,' she said, 'that when he's beating you, it's because he's been fucking me so beautifully, all night, that he can't bear the sight of your disappointed little face in the morning.'

The sound of her name coming out of the mulatto's mouth made Inés catch her breath with a loud cluck. Thereafter the words sliced through her with the ferocity of blasted glass. The arrogance of her own anger disappeared. She felt the shame of being stripped naked in public with all eyes on her.

Marisa saw the fight go out of her and watched the sag in Inés's shoulders with some satisfaction. She felt no pity; she'd suffered much worse when she'd lived in America. In fact the thin white hand with which Inés now held her side, no longer able to disguise the pain, only made Marisa think of other possibilities. Fate had brought them together and now it was up to one to shape the destiny of the other.

11

A group of workmen had formed around the section of the building where Fernando had pinpointed his wife's position from the sound of her mobile phone. Fernando was on his haunches, with his hands clasped over the top of his head, trying to exert additional gravitational force, as if there was the possibility that more tragedy might carry him away like a child's lost helium-filled balloon.

The crane loomed over the scene with its wrist-thick steel cable, taut and creaking. There were workmen on ladders using motorized hand-held saws, capable of ripping through concrete and steel with a noise that went through Falcón taking shreds with it. They had inserted hydraulic props and thick scaffolding planks to keep the collapsed floors apart as they carved out a tunnel. Chunks of concrete were coughed from the hole within clouds of dust, and showers of sparks spewed out as the saws' teeth bit into steel. The goggled workmen, grey as ghosts, plunged further in until the unbearable sound stopped and there was a call for more props and planks. The sun beat down. The sweat tracked dark rivulets through the grey dust on the workmen's faces. Once the props and planks were inserted the saws started up again, making all humans aware of the savagery of their metal teeth. The workmen were off the ladders now, kneeling on pads strapped to their knees, staring into the tangled skeleton of the building, embraced by claws of steel rods jutting from the shattered concrete.

He knew he should move away, that the sight of the confused guts of the building was not good preparation for the task at hand, but Falcón was caught up in the drama and was feeding a profound sense of anger at the tragedy. Only Ramírez calling wrenched him out of his distraction.

'We're getting reports of a blue transit van that was parked outside the front of the building yesterday morning,' said Ramírez. 'There seems to be confusion about the numbers of people in it. Some say two, others three and still others, four. They brought in tool boxes, a plastic box of some sort of electrical supplies and insulation tubing, carried in rolls over their shoulders. Nobody remembers any company name on the side of the van.'

'And it all went into the mosque?'

'There's confusion there, too,' said Ramírez. 'Most of the people we're talking to don't live in the building, they were just passers-by. Some didn't know there was a mosque in the basement. We're getting snapshots of what happened. I've got Pérez working on the residents list. He's down at the hospital. Serrano and Baena are working the surrounding blocks and people in the street. Where's Cristina?'

'She should still be working those blocks on Calle

Los Romeros,' said Falcón. 'What we need to find is someone who was *inside* the mosque in the last forty-eight hours to corroborate what we're hearing about on the outside. What about that woman, Esperanza, who gave Comisario Elvira the list – didn't she leave a number? Call her and get some names and addresses. Those women must know.'

'Hasn't anybody from the Moroccan community approached the Comisario yet?'

'Somebody turned up with the Mayor,' said Falcón. 'You know what it's like. They've got to contain the media before they can give us any practical help.'

'You remember that mosque they wanted to build over in Los Bermejales?' said Ramírez. 'A huge place, big enough for seven hundred worshippers. There was a protest group organized by the locals called Los Vecinos de Los Bermejales.'

'That's right, they had a website, too, called www.mezquitanogracias.com. There were a lot of accusations about xenophobia, racism and anti-Muslim activity, especially after March 11th.'

'Maybe we should look up some of the personalities from that dispute,' said Ramírez. 'Or is that too obvious?'

'Keep working on what happened inside and outside the building in the last forty-eight hours,' said Falcón. 'In the end there are two possibilities: explosives were brought here by terrorists and accidentally exploded, or an anti-Muslim group has planted a bomb and set it off. There are a lot of complications within those scenarios, but those are the two basic concepts. Let's work with the information we find, rather than getting distracted by the possibilities.'

155

Falcón hung up. The saws had stopped. The workmen were shovelling out rubble by hand. Two more props, planks and lights were called for. Men ran up the ladders with the equipment. Props were passed in. Torches were trained into the hole. A single saw ripped into some steel and stopped. A length of metal rod was flung out followed by more rubble. Four paramedics leaned against their ambulance, waiting for their turn in the drama. Two cradle stretchers with straps were brought to the foot of the ladders by the rescue teams. Fernando was concentrating on his breathing, under orders from his trauma counsellor. There was a shout for a doctor. A Médico Forense stepped up the ladder with his bag and crawled down the tunnel. There was silence, apart from the rumble of the insulated diesel generators. The diggers had stopped work. The drivers were out of their cabs watching. There was a collective need to wring some hope out of this calamitous day.

Another shout, this time for a stretcher. The doctor backed out on all fours and came down the ladder, while two men from the rescue services dragged the stretcher up the other ladder. Fernando came off his haunches and in seconds was on the doctor, holding him by the sleeves of his shirt. The doctor grasped Fernando by the shoulders and spoke directly into his eyes. The tension in their strange embrace made them look like judoists, struggling for the upper hand. Fernando's hands fell to his sides. The doctor put his arm around him and beckoned the counsellor. Fernando leaned into him like a lost child. The doctor spoke to the trauma counsellor over Fernando's shoulder.

The doctor trotted over to the paramedics, who

radioed through to the hospital. He talked directly with the emergency room. The paramedics reversed the ambulance up to the ladders, opened the double doors, prepared the trolley with a head, neck and spine immobilizer, turned on the oxygen, charged the defibrillator.

The workmen, who'd plunged into the hole after the doctor had backed out, now called the rescue workers in with the stretcher. The Médico Forense joined Falcón, just as Calderón came round from the front of the building.

'Have we got a survivor in there?' asked Calderón.

'The woman is dead,' said the doctor, 'but her child is hanging on. She's breathing and there's a thready pulse. The mother seems to have fallen with her body protecting the child, as much as possible, from the debris falling on top of them. The problem is to get the girl out. The mother's back is facing the rescue workers, so they've got to lift the child up and over her body and there's no room in there. If the child has a spinal injury, just the movement could cause permanent paralysis, but if she stays there much longer she'll die.'

The workmen roared from the mouth of the hole and held their thumbs up. The rescue workers slid the steel cradle stretcher out, mounted it on the ladder's sliders and lowered it to the paramedics, who lifted the girl out, on the count, and fitted her into the immobilizer. Two television crews came running, pursued by local police. The Médico Forense made a full report to Calderón. The pneumatic drills, saws and diggers started up again as if galvanized by this thin slice of hope. Falcón got into the ambulance cab. The trolley was lifted into the back, followed by Fernando. A cameraman was pushed back roughly by one of the workmen. The door closed on a woman's microphone. The driver leapt into his seat and set the siren off. He drove slowly over the rough ground until he got back on to the tarmac. Photojournalists stormed the side and back of the ambulance, holding cameras up to the windows and flashing away. The lurid lights, hysterical siren and the sprinting journalists left pedestrians gaping and slack-faced.

The news of a survivor travelled faster than the ambulance and there was a media scrum, battling it out with a dozen local policemen and hospital orderlies, at the entrance to the hospital. The ambulance ramp was clear and they got the girl out and through the swing doors before the newsmen could get near her. Fernando was sucked in after her. The media rounded on Falcón, who they'd seen in the ambulance cab, and he steadied their hysteria by informing them that the girl had been removed from the destroyed building showing signs of life. A doctor would make a full statement once he'd completed his examination. Falcón held up his hand and pushed back the barrage of questions that followed.

Ten minutes later he'd picked up his car from the Forensic Institute and was easing his way out through a gaggle of journalists still desperate for his final words. He crossed the river and went into the old Expo ground. He found Informáticalidad in an office that fronted a large warehouse on Calle Albert Einstein. He showed his police ID to the woman in reception and told her he wanted an immediate interview with Pedro Plata in connection with a murder investigation. He gave her his stoniest policeman's stare and she phoned through. Sr Plata was in a board meeting but would make himself

158

available in a few minutes. She took him through security to an office with glass walls on all sides. The receptionist was still the only visible person. There was a lack of movement in the building, as if business was slow, even dead.

Pedro Plata arrived with the receptionist, who set down two coffees and left. He had only been responsible for buying the property so could offer no help in explaining how it had been used.

'Any reason why you bought it rather than rented it?'

'Only if you assure me this is not going to get back to the tax authorities, or be used against this company in any way.'

'My job is finding murderers.'

'We had some black money to get rid of.'

'And its use wasn't discussed at a board meeting?'

'Not one I attended,' said Plata. 'It was Diego Torres's idea, he's the Human Resources Director, you'd best talk to him.'

More time leaked past. The chill of the air conditioning and his exposure in the glass office made him feel like an Arctic zoo animal. Diego Torres arrived and before he'd even sat down Falcón asked him how they'd used the apartment.

'We try to encourage our employees to think creatively, not just about our business but business in general,' said Torres. 'Where will the next opportunities come from? Is there another strand that we can attach to our core business? Is there another business out there that could improve our own, or help it to grow? Is there a totally different project that could be worth investing in? These sorts of things.'

'And you think you can achieve that by investing in a small apartment, in an anonymous block, in a poor neighbourhood of Seville?'

'That was a conscious decision,' said Torres. 'Our employees complained that they never had time to think creatively, they were always too busy with the work at hand. They came to us demanding "brainstorming time". A lot of companies offer this and it normally consists of sending employees away to an expensive country club, where they attend meetings and seminars, listen to gurus spouting common sense and charging a fortune, interspersed with tennis, swimming and staying up until five in the morning partying.'

'They must have been very disappointed by your solution,' said Falcón. 'How many employees did you lose?'

'None from that project, but there's always a certain amount of churn in the sales teams. It's hard work with demanding targets. We pay well, but we expect results. A lot of young guys think they can handle the pressure, but they burn out, or lose their drive. It's a young person's business. There are no sales reps over thirty.'

'You're telling me you didn't lose anybody when you showed them that apartment in El Cerezo?'

'We're not stupid, Inspector Jefe,' said Torres. 'We gave them a sweetener. The idea was that they should take the brainstorming seriously. We put them in a place outside their normal environment, with no distractions, not even a decent café to go to, so that they would concentrate on the task. They went in pairs and we swapped the people around. They were told it was a finite project, three months maximum, and they wouldn't have to spend more than four hours at a time in the apartment. They were also told that they would be a part of any of their projects which received board approval.'

'Was that the sweetener?'

'We're not that tough on them,' said Torres. 'The sweetener was a fully paid break in a beach hotel, with golf and tennis, during the Feria – and they wouldn't have to do any work. We let them bring their girl-friends, too.'

'And boyfriends?'

Torres blinked, as if that little comment had short-circuited something in his brain. Falcón thought Torres might be inferring something 'inappropriate' from his remark until he remembered that only men had been seen going into the apartment.

'You *do* employ women, don't you, Sr Torres?'

'The receptionist who showed you in here is . . .'

'How do you recruit, Sr Torres?'

'We advertise at business schools and through recruitment agencies.'

'Give me some names and telephone numbers,' said Falcón, handing him his notebook. 'How many people have you fired in the last year?'

'None.'

'Two years?'

'None. We don't fire people. They leave.'

'It's cheaper that way,' said Falcón. 'I'd like a list of all the people who have left your employ in the last year, and I'd also like the names and addresses of all the *men* who frequented that apartment in Calle Los Romeros.'

'Why?'

'We have to know whether they saw anything while they were there, especially in the last week.'

'It might not be so easy for you to interview my sales reps.'

'You'll have to *make* it easy. We're looking for people who are responsible for the deaths of four children and five adults . . . so far. And the first forty-eight hours of an investigation are critical.'

'When would you like to start?'

'Two members of my squad will begin contacting your sales reps as soon as you've given me their names and phone numbers,' said Falcón. 'And why, by the way, did you insist on your employees being there in the hours of daylight?'

'Those are the hours they work anyway. They sell from nine in the morning until eight at night while businesses are open. Then there's the paperwork, team meetings, course studies, product information classes. Twelve-hour days are the short ones.'

'Let me have a list with addresses and phone numbers of all the board members, too.'

'Now?'

'Along with those other lists I asked for,' said Falcón. 'I *am* busy, too, Sr Torres. So if you could bring them to me in the next ten minutes it would be appreciated.'

Torres stood and went to shake Falcón's hand.

'I'd like you to bring me the lists, Sr Torres,' said Falcón. 'I'll have more questions by then.'

Torres left. Falcón went to the toilet; there was an electronic plaque above each urinal, which streamed quotes from the Bible and inspirational business maxims. Informáticalidad extracted the best out of its employees

162

by embracing them in a culture not unlike a religious sect.

The receptionist was waiting for him outside the toilets. It looked as if she'd been sent to make sure he didn't roam too freely around the corridors, despite all the offices being controlled by security key pads. She took him back to Torres, who was waiting with the lists.

'Is Informáticalidad part of a holding company?' asked Falcón.

'We're in the high-technology division of a Spanish company based in Madrid called Horizonte. They are owned by a US investment company called I4IT.'

'Who are they?'

'Who knows?' said Torres. 'The I4 bit is Indianapolis Investment Interests Incorporated and IT is Information Technology. I think they started out investing only in Hi-Tech, but they're broader based than that now.'

Torres walked him back to reception.

'How many ideas and projects did your reps come up with while they were in Calle Los Romeros?'

'Fifteen ideas, which have already been incorporated into our working practices, and four projects which are still in the planning stage.'

'Have you ever heard of a website called www.vomit.org?'

'Never,' said Torres, and let the door slowly close.

Back in his car Falcón checked his mobiles for calls. Informáticalidad's building, a steel cage covered in tinted glass, reflected its surroundings. On top of the building were four banners with company logos: Informáticalidad, Quirúrgicalidad, Ecográficalidad and finally a slightly larger placard featuring a huge pair of spectacles with a horizon running through them and above, the word Optivisión. High technology, robotic surgical instruments, ultrasound machines and laser equipment for correcting visual defects. This company had access to the internal workings of the body. They could see inside you, remove and implant things and make sure you saw the world the way they saw it. It disturbed Falcón.

12

Seville – Tuesday, 6th June 2006, 15.45 hrs

As Falcón pulled away, car rippling along the glass façade of the building, he put a call through to Mark Flowers, who was euphemistically known as a Communications Officer in the US Consulate in Seville. He was a CIA operative who, after 9/11, had been pulled out of retirement, posted to Madrid and transferred to Seville. Falcón had met him during an investigation back in 2002. They had stayed in touch, or rather Falcón had become one of Flowers' sources and, in return, received intelligence and a more direct and proactive line to the FBI.

'Returning your call, Mark,' said Falcón.

'We should talk.'

'Have you got anything for me?'

'Nothing. It came out of the blue. I'm working on stuff.'

'Can you get some information for me on a company called I4IT, that's Indianapolis Investment Interests Incorporated in Information Technology.'

'Sure,' said Flowers. 'When can we meet?'

'Tonight. Late. Our people want to "interview" me,'

165

said Falcón. 'If you come afterwards you might be able to give me some advice.'

Falcón hung up. The radio news gave its latest summary of events: a group called the Mártires Islámicos para la Liberación de Andalucía had called both TVE and RNE to claim responsibility for the attack. El Corte Inglés had been evacuated and there was a stampede in the Calle Tetuán because of a bomb scare. All roads out of Seville, especially the motorway south towards Jerez de la Frontera, were jammed with traffic.

Falcón had to resist the image of a vast dust cloud on the outskirts of Seville, thick with panicked cattle beneath.

As he drove back across the river his mobile vibrated; Ramírez wanting to know where he was.

'We've found somebody who's a regular at the mosque,' he said. 'He goes there every evening after work, for prayers. We'll see you in the pre-school.'

Falcón came into the barrio of El Cerezo from the north, to avoid any traffic around the hospital. In the pre-school he photocopied the lists of personnel from Informáticalidad and gave them to Ramírez with orders for two members of the squad to start interviewing the sales reps to see if they'd noticed anything. Ramírez introduced the Moroccan man, who was called Said Harrouch. He was a cook, born in 1958 in Larache in northern Morocco.

The demolition work was too loud for them to talk in any of the classrooms, none of which had any glass in the windows, so they moved to the man's apart-ment nearby. Harrouch's wife made them mint tea and they sat in a room facing away from the destroyed building.

'You're a cook for a manufacturing company in the Polígono Industrial Calonge,' said Ramírez. 'What hours do you work?'

'Seven in the morning until five in the afternoon,' he said. 'They let me go back home when they heard about the bomb.'

'Do you go to the mosque at a regular time?'

'I manage to get there some time between half past five and a quarter to six.'

'Every day?'

'On the weekends I go five times a day.'

'Do you just pray, or do you spend time there?'

'At the weekends there's tea and I'll sit around and talk.'

The man was calm. He sat back from the table with his hands clasped across his stomach. He blinked slowly with long lashes and no wariness of either policeman.

'How long have you lived in Seville?'

'Nearly sixteen years,' he said. 'I came over in 1990 to work on the Expo site. I never went back.'

'Do you like living here in this neighbourhood?'

'I preferred living in the old city,' he said. 'It was more like home.'

'How are the people here?'

'You mean the Spanish people?' he asked. 'They're all right, most of them. Some of them don't like so many of us Moroccans being here.'

'You don't have to be diplomatic,' said Ramírez. 'Tell us how it really is.'

'After the Madrid train bombings a lot of people are very suspicious of us,' said Harrouch. 'They might have been told that not every North African is a terrorist, but it doesn't help when there are so many of us about.

167

The Imam has done his best to explain to local people that terrorism is a problem with an extreme minority, and that he himself does not agree with their radical interpretations of Islam, and does not approve of it in his mosque. It hasn't helped. They are still suspicious. I tell them that even in Morocco you would struggle to find anyone who actively approves of what these few fanatics are doing, but they don't believe us. Of course, if you go to a teahouse in Tangier you will hear people getting angry about what the Americans and the Israelis are doing. You will see protests on the streets about the plight of the Palestinians. But that is just talk and demonstration. It doesn't mean we're all about to strap bombs to our chests and go out and kill. Our own people were killed in the suicide bombings in Casablanca in May 2003 and Muslims died on those trains in Madrid in 2004 and in London in 2005, but they don't remember that.'

'That's the nature of terror, isn't it, Sr Harrouch?' said Falcón. 'The terrorist wants people to know that this can happen in any place, at any time, to anybody – Christian, Muslim, Hindu or Buddhist. This seems to be the state we are in now, here in Seville. People can no longer feel safe in their homes. What we want to find out, as soon as possible, is: who wants us to be terrified or, if that's too difficult, why they want us to be terrified.'

'But, of course, everybody will assume it is us,' said Harrouch, putting his fingertips to his chest. 'As I left work this morning, I was insulted in the street by people who can only think in one way when they hear that a bomb has gone off.'

'On 11th March the government automatically thought it was ETA,' said Ramírez.

'We know that there are anti-Muslim groups,' said Falcón.

'We've all heard of VOMIT, for instance,' said Harrouch. Then, registering the policemen's surprise: 'We spend a lot of time on the internet. That's how we communicate with our families back in Morocco.'

'We only found out about it this morning,' said Falcón.

'But it isn't directed at you, is it?' said Harrouch. 'It's designed to show that Islam is a religion of hate, which is not true. We see VOMIT as just another way that the West has devised to set out to humiliate us.'

'But it isn't *the West* that has created that website,' said Ramírez. 'It's another fanatical minority within the West.'

'The fact is, Sr Harrouch, it's going to take time for us to reach the basement where the mosque was located,' said Falcón, drawing the discussion back to business. 'We're going to have to wait days for any forensic information from the site of the actual bomb. What we have to rely on, for the moment, is witness accounts. Who was seen going in and out of that building over the last seventy-two hours. So far we have had a sighting of two vehicles: a white Peugeot Partner with two Moroccan men, who were seen delivering cardboard boxes —'

'Of sugar,' said Harrouch, suddenly animated. 'I was there when they brought it in yesterday. It was sugar. It was clearly printed on the sides of the boxes. And they had plastic carrier bags of mint. It was for the tea.'

'Did you know those two men?' asked Ramírez. 'Had you seen them before?'

'No, I didn't know them,' he said. 'I'd never seen them before.'

'So who did know them? Who did they make contact with?'

'Imam Abdelkrim Benaboura.'

'What did they do with this sugar and mint?'

'They took it into the storeroom at the back of the mosque.'

'Were these men introduced to anybody?'

'No.'

'Do you know where they came from?' asked Falcón.

'Someone said they were from Madrid.'

'How long did they stay in the mosque talking to the Imam?'

'They were still there when I left at seven o'clock.'

'Could they have spent the night there?'

'It's possible. People have slept in the mosque before.'

'Do you remember when they arrived?' asked Ramírez.

'About ten minutes after I came in from work, so about a quarter to six.'

'Can you tell us exactly what they did?'

'They came in, each carrying a box with a carrier bag of mint on top. They asked for the Imam. He came out of his office and showed them the storeroom. They stowed the boxes and then went back outside and brought another two boxes in.'

'Then what?'

'They left.'

'Empty-handed?'

'I think so,' said Harrouch. 'But they came back a few minutes later. I think they went off to park their car. When they returned they went into the Imam's office and they hadn't come out again by the time I left.'

'Did you hear anything of their conversation?'

Harrouch shook his head. Falcón sensed the man's nausea at the endless questions about seemingly unimportant detail. Harrouch somehow felt he was compromising these two men, who he believed had just delivered sugar and nothing more. Falcón told him not to worry about the questions, they were asked only to see if they squared with other witness accounts.

'Did you hear any talk of other outsiders who'd turned up that morning?' asked Ramírez.

'Outsiders?'

'Workmen, delivery people . . . that sort of thing.'

'The electricians came at some stage. Something had gone wrong with the electrics on Saturday night. We were in the dark, with just candles, all Sunday and when I came in from work yesterday all the lights were back on. I don't know what happened or what work was done. You'll have to ask someone who was there in the morning.'

Ramírez asked him for some names and checked them off against the list of men given to Elvira by the Spanish woman, Esperanza. The first three names Harrouch gave him were on the list and therefore probably dead in the mosque. The fourth name lived in an apartment in a nearby street.

'How well do you know the Imam?'

'He's been with us nearly two years. He reads a lot. I've heard his apartment is full of books. But he still gives us as much of his time as he can,' said Harrouch. 'I told you he was not a radical. He never said anything that could be construed as extreme, and he even made his position clear on suicide bombing: that in his view the Koran did not regard it as permissible. And remember, there were Spanish

171

converts to Islam in the mosque, who would not tolerate anything extreme so . . .'

'If he was preaching radical Islam to younger people,' said Ramírez, 'do you think you would know about it?'

'In a neighbourhood like this it wouldn't be possible to keep it secret.'

'Apart from these two men who delivered the sugar and mint, have you ever seen the Imam with any other strangers? I mean people from out of town, or from abroad?'

'I saw him with Spanish people. He was very aware of the image of Islam in the light of what has been happening in the last few years. He made efforts to communicate with Catholic priests and spoke at their meetings to reassure them that not all North Africans were terrorists.'

'Do you know anything about his history?'

'He's Algerian originally. He arrived here from Tunis. He must have spent some time in Egypt, because he talked about it a lot and he's mentioned studying in Khartoum.'

'How did he learn Spanish?' asked Falcón. 'The countries you mention have either French, or English, as the alternative to Arabic.'

'He learnt it here. The converts taught him,' said Harrouch. 'He was a good linguist, he spoke quite a few –'

'What other languages?' asked Ramírez.

'German. He spoke German,' said Harrouch, who'd gone back on the defensive.

'Does that mean he'd spent time in Germany?' asked Ramírez.

'I suppose he did, but that doesn't have to mean anything,' said Harrouch. 'Just because the 9/11 bombers came from Hamburg, it doesn't mean that any Muslim who's been to Germany is also a radical. I hope you're not forgetting that it was the mosque that was bombed and there were more than ten people in it, and most of them were older men, with wives and children, and not young, radical, extreme bomb-makers. I would say that we were the *target* of an attack . . .'

'All right, Sr Harrouch,' said Falcón, calming him. 'You should know that we're looking at all the possibilities. You mentioned VOMIT. Are you aware of any other anti-Muslim groups who you think would go to such extremes?'

'There were some very unpleasant demonstrations against the building of our mosque in Los Bermejales,' said Harrouch. 'Maybe you don't remember – they slaughtered a pig on the proposed site of the mosque back in May last year. There's a very vociferous protest group.'

'We know about them,' said Ramírez. 'We'll be taking a close look at their activities.'

'Did you ever feel that you were being watched, or under some kind of surveillance?' asked Falcón. 'Has anybody joined the mosque recently, who you didn't know or who, in your opinion, behaved strangely?'

'People are suspicious of us, but I don't think anybody was watching us.'

Ramírez checked the descriptions of the two men from the Peugeot Partner with the men Harrouch had seen bringing boxes into the mosque. Harrouch answered with his mind elsewhere. They got up to leave.

'Now I remember, there was something else that

happened last week,' said Harrouch. 'Someone told me that the mosque had been inspected by the council. Because we're technically a public building, we have to conform to certain rules about fire and safety, and two men came round last week, without any warning, and went through everything – drains, plumbing, electrics – the lot.'

13

'What did you make of him?' Falcón asked Ramírez as they made their way back to the pre-school for a meeting with Comisario Elvira and Juez Calderón

'The difficulty with these people is not disentangling the truth from the lies. I don't think Sr Harrouch is a liar. He's been an immigrant for sixteen years and he's developed the knack for telling you the story which will give him the least amount of trouble, and makes his people appear in the best possible light,' said Ramírez. 'He says the Imam has never preached a radical word in his life, but he faltered over the Imam's linguistic ability. Why wasn't he happy about revealing the languages the Imam could speak? Because it was German. Not only the Hamburg connection, but it also means he's moved around Europe. It's making the Imam look more suspicious.'

'He was straight about the two young guys turning up with their cardboard boxes.'

'Of *sugar*,' said Ramírez. 'He was very emphatic about that. He was reluctant to reveal anything more about them, though. He wanted to be able to say he knew them, but he couldn't. He wanted to be able to stand up for them in some way. But if they're just shifting sugar around, what's the problem? Why does he feel the need to protect them?'

'Loyalty to other Muslims,' said Falcón.

'Or repercussions?' said Ramírez.

'Even if they don't know each other, there's a sense of allegiance,' said Falcón. 'Sr Harrouch is a decent, hardworking man and he'd like us to think that all his people are the same. When something like this bombing happens they feel embattled, and the instinct is to put up the defences all around, even if he ends up defending the sort of people he may abhor.'

Elvira and Calderón had been joined by Gregorio from the CNI.

'There have been some developments in Madrid,' said Elvira. 'Gregorio will explain.'

'We've been working on the notes found in the margins of the copy of the Koran, from the Peugeot Partner,' said Gregorio. 'In the meantime, copies of the notes were faxed up to Madrid and they made comparisons with the handwriting of the van's owner, Mohammed Soumaya, and his nephew Trabelsi Amar. They don't match.'

'Do the notes reveal anything?' asked Calderón. 'Are there any extremist views?'

'Our expert on the Koran says that the owner of this book has made interesting, rather than radical, interpretations of the text,' said Gregorio.

'Have you found Trabelsi Amar yet?' asked Ramírez.

'He was still in Madrid,' said Gregorio, nodding. 'He was just keeping out of the way of his uncle until he got the van back, which was supposed to be this

176

evening. When he heard about the bomb he went into hiding, which was obviously not part of the plan, because the best hiding place he could think of was a friend's house, not some prearranged safe house. The local police picked him up a couple of hours ago.'

'Has he identified the people he lent the van to?' asked Ramírez.

'Yes. He's very scared,' said Gregorio. 'The CGI's antiterrorist squad in Madrid say he hasn't been behaving like a terrorist at all. He's been happy to tell them the whole story.'

'Let's start with the names,' said Ramírez.

'The shaven-headed guy is Djamel Hammad, thirty-one years old, born in Tlemcen in Algeria. His friend is Smail Saoudi, thirty years old, born Tiaret in Algeria. Both were resident in Morocco and still should be.'

'What sort of records have they got?'

'Those are their original names. They've operated under a lot of pseudonyms. They were medium- to high-risk terror suspects, by which I mean they were not likely to actually carry out attacks, but they have been suspected of document forgery, recce and logistical work. They both have relatives who have been active in the GIA – the Armed Islamic Group.'

'And how did Trabelsi Amar get to know them?'

'They're all illegal immigrants. They came across the straits together, on the same shipment. Hammad and Saoudi made him their friend. They got him to Madrid and helped him with his documents. Then they called in the favour.'

'Didn't he find their slickness . . . suspicious?' asked Calderón.

177

'It was convenient for him not to,' said Gregorio. 'Trabelsi Amar is not very bright.'

'What's the story with the van?' asked Ramírez.

'Amar has been working for his uncle making deliveries. He also did a few things on the side, to make himself some extra cash. He ran errands, some of them were for Hammad and Saoudi. Then they asked to borrow the van; the first time for an afternoon, the second time for a whole day. It all happened gradually, so that when they asked to borrow the van to go to Seville for three days and said they'd give him €250, Trabelsi Amar just saw the money.'

'How did he explain that to his Uncle Mohammed?' asked Ramírez.

'He rented the van from him for € 30 a day,' said Gregorio. 'He might not be bright, but he could still work out that he didn't have to do anything and he'd be € 160 up on the deal.'

'So presumably he knows where Hammad and Saoudi live.'

'They're searching the apartment as we speak.'

'When exactly did Amar go into hiding?' asked Ramírez. 'When he heard about the bomb, or once it was reported that the Peugeot Partner had been found?'

'As soon as he heard about the bomb,' said Gregorio.

'So he'd probably worked out already that his new friends weren't just ordinary guys.'

'What about their relationship with the Imam Abdelkrim Benaboura,' asked Falcón, 'apart from the fact that they were all Algerians?'

'The only connection we can see at the moment was that Benaboura was born in Tlemcen, which doesn't mean much.'

'We've found out more about the Imam from a member of the mosque than we have from the CNI and the CGI put together,' said Falcón.

'We still don't have the authority to access any more information,' said Gregorio. 'And that includes Juan, who, as you've probably gathered, is a very senior officer.'

'The Imam is a player of some sort,' said Ramírez. 'I'm sure of it.'

'What about this group, the MILA, who, according to the television news, have claimed responsibility for the blast?' asked Falcón.

'It's not a group we've ever heard of having an active terrorist dimension,' said Gregorio. 'We've heard about their intention to "liberate" Andalucía, but we've never taken it seriously. With the current military set-up in this country it's just not possible for anyone but a major power to secure a region of Spain for themselves. The Basques haven't achieved it and they don't even have to invade.'

'And what did the CGI in Madrid know about Hammad and Saoudi being in Spain?' asked Calderón.

'They didn't,' said Gregorio. 'It's not as easy as it sounds to trace unknown radicals in a huge, constantly changing immigrant population, some of whom are legal and others who've been smuggled across the straits. We know, for instance, that some of these people come over, perform two or three tasks in this country and then move on, to be replaced by others from France, Germany or the Netherlands. Quite often they have no idea of the purpose of what they're doing. They deliver a package, drive a person somewhere, raise some money from stolen bank cards, travel on a train at certain times to report on passenger numbers and time spent at how many stations, or they're asked to look at a building and report on its security situation. Even if we catch them and extract their task from them, which is not easy, all we end up with is a little strip of footage that could be one of a hundred operations that might make up a major attack, or might just be something that ends up on the cutting-room floor.'

'Does anyone have any opinion about what Hammad and Saoudi might have been doing?' asked Falcón.

'We don't know enough. We hope to know more after we've searched their apartment,' said Gregorio.

'What about the hood and the Islamic sash?' said Ramírez. 'Isn't that what operatives wear when they videotape themselves before a suicide mission?'

'No comment from the CGI on that,' said Gregorio. 'Based on the interview with Trabelsi Amar, they think the guys were logistical and nothing more.'

Ramírez gave a report on the deliveries to the mosque, the council visit last week, the power cut on Saturday night and the electricians' repair work performed on Monday morning. Falcón held back on disclosing his findings from the interview with Diego Torres of Informáticalidad until they had more information from interviews with the sales reps.

'Do we know anything more about the explosive used?' asked Calderón.

'The bomb squad have given me this report,' said Elvira. 'Based on their preliminary investigation of the site, the distance from the epicentre to the furthest flung pieces of debris, and the extent of the destruction of the first three floors of the building, their conservative estimate is that three times the quantity of hexogen was exploded than was necessary, if the intention was to destroy the apartment block.'

'Do they deduce anything from that?' asked Calderón. 'Or is that left up to our, inexpert, assuming?'

'That's what they're prepared to put in writing at the moment,' said Elvira. 'Verbally, they tell me that to destroy a building of this size, with demolition knowledge easily found on the internet, they would need as little as twenty kilos of hexogen. They say that hexogen is commonly used in demolition work, but primarily to shear through solid steel girders. Twenty kilos expertly positioned in an ordinary reinforced concrete building would wreck the whole block, not just the section that was actually destroyed. They deduce from this that the explosive was located in one place in the basement of the building, more towards the back than the front, hence the damage done to the pre-school. They thought that it could have been as much as one hundred kilos of hexogen that exploded.'

'Well, that sounds like enough to start a serious bombing campaign in Seville,' said Calderón. 'And if this is a group with plans to liberate the whole of Andalucía . . .'

'You probably haven't seen the latest news,' said Elvira, 'but we're on red alert all over the region. They've evacuated the cathedral in Cordoba, and the Alhambra and Generalife in Granada. There are now special patrols going through the tourist resorts on the Costa del Sol, and there are more than twenty roadblocks along the N340. The Navy are off the coast and there are Air Force fighters on all major airstrips. More than forty helicopters are running up and down the main arterial routes through Andalucía. Zapatero is taking this threat very seriously indeed.'

'Well, he has the demise of his predecessor's political ambitions as an example,' said Calderón. 'And nobody wants to be the Prime Minister who lost Andalucía to the Muslims after more than five hundred years of Spanish rule.'

They weren't quite ready to laugh at Calderón's cynicism. The sense of all that activity described by Elvira was too powerful, and, as if to reinforce his words, a helicopter passed rapidly overhead, like the latest despatch to a new crisis point. Falcón broke the silence.

'The CGI antiterrorist squad in Madrid think that Hammad and Saoudi were providing logistical support for an unknown cell that was going to carry out an attack, or series of attacks. Clearly, a delivery of some sort was made on Monday 5th June. A single hood and sash were found in the delivery vehicle, possibly indicating that either Hammad or Saoudi might become operatives. It also might indicate that one of them was going to return the van to Madrid, so that Trabelsi Amar had his van back as arranged.

'What history can show us is that, prior to the March 11th attacks in Madrid, two cell members went up to Avilés to pick up explosives on the 28th and 29th February. They allowed themselves a full *ten* days to prepare for the attacks. In our scenario, here, we are being asked to believe that the hexogen in raw, powder form was delivered on Monday, and that on the same night they started preparing bombs so that they were all ready to go on Tuesday morning. Then at approximately 8.30 a.m. there was an accident and the explosion occurred. I realize that this is not impossible, and

in the history of terrorism there probably exists an inci-
dence of delivery, preparation and attack being carried
out within twenty-four hours, but if you're a group planning the liberation of Andalucía this doesn't seem very
likely.'

'What's the scenario you envisage?' asked Gregorio.

'I don't. I'm just picking holes. I was trying to find
a line of logic, but there were too many breaks. I don't
want our investigation to go down a single path within
the first twelve hours of the incident,' said Falcón.
'We're probably going to have to wait two or three
days to get forensic information from the mosque, and
until that time I think we should keep both possibilities open: that there was an accident in the bomb-
making procedure, or that this was an attack on the
mosque.'

'Why would someone want to attack the mosque?'
asked Calderón.

'Revenge, extreme xenophobia, political or business
motivation, or perhaps a combination of all four,' said
Falcón. 'Terror is just a tool to bring about change.
Look at the havoc wreaked by this bomb. Terror focuses
people's attention and creates opportunities for
powerful people. The population of this city is already
fleeing. With that sort of panic, unimaginable things
become possible.'

'The only way to contain panic,' said Comisario
Elvira, 'is to show people that we are in control.'

'Even if we aren't,' said Juez Calderón. 'Even if we
don't have the first idea where to look.'

'Whoever is behind this, whether it's Islamic militants or "other forces", they've planned their media
assault,' said Falcón. 'The *ABC* received the Abdullah

183

Azzam text in a letter with a Seville stamp. TVE tells us that the MILA have called to claim responsibility.'

'Would they be claiming responsibility for blowing up a mosque and killing their own people?' asked Calderón.

'That's an everyday occurrence in Baghdad,' said Elvira.

'If you send something like Azzam's text to the *ABC* then you're expecting to launch an attack imminently . . . not even within twenty-four hours,' said Gregorio. 'As far as I know, Islamic militants have never advertised their exact intentions; all the big ones have come out of the blue, with the intention of killing and maiming as many people as possible.'

Gregorio took a call on his mobile and asked to leave.

'We've had this preliminary report from the bomb squad about the explosion,' said Falcón, 'but what about the explosive? Where does it come from and what are all these different names for it?'

'Hexogen is the German name, cyclonite is American, RDX is British and I think the Italians call it T4,' said Elvira. 'They might each have signatures, which enables them to identify the origin, but they're not going to tell us.'

'We could use some shots of Hammad and Saoudi,' said Ramírez.

'If they're into document fraud there'll probably be a load of photographs in their apartment in Madrid,' said Falcón. 'Has there been an update on the demolition work outside yet?'

'They're still saying forty-eight hours minimum, and that's if they don't come across anything to slow them down.'

Juez Calderón took a call, announced the discovery of another body and left. Falcón made eye contact with Ramírez and he left the room.

'Still no news on the CGI?' asked Falcón. 'I expected to be pooling resources and efforts with the antiterrorist unit, and the only person we've seen is Inspector Jefe Ramón Barros, who doesn't say very much and appears humiliated.'

'I'm told that their job is more to do with gathering data at this stage,' said Comisario Elvira.

'What about some lower level people to help with the interviewing?'

'Not possible.'

'This sounds like something you can't talk about . . .'

'All I'm going to say is that since March 11th one aspect of counterterrorism measures has been to check that our own organizations are clean,' said Elvira.

'Don't tell me,' said Falcón.

'The Seville branch is under investigation. Nobody is giving any detail, but as far as I can gather, the CNI ran a test on the Seville antiterrorism unit and did not get the right result. They believe they have been compromised in some way. There are some high-level discussions going on now as to whether they should be allowed to participate in this investigation or not. You're not going to get any active help from the Madrid CGI either. They're working flat-out on their own informer network, and they've got the whole Hammad and Saoudi mess to sort through.'

'Will we be getting informer feedback from the Seville CGI network?'

'Not for the moment,' said Elvira. 'I'm sorry to be so reticent, but the situation is delicate. I don't know what the members of the antiterrorism unit are being told to make them believe that they are not under suspicion, but the CNI are trying to play it both ways. They don't want the mole, if he exists, to know that they're on to him, but neither do they want him endangering the investigation without them knowing who he is. Ideally, they want to find him and then release the CGI into the investigation and give themselves the chance of using him.'

'That sounds like a risky manoeuvre.'

'That's why it's taking so long to decide. The politicians are involved now,' said Elvira.

Outside, the grind of machinery had become the acceptable ambient noise. Men moved like aliens in a grey lunar landscape over the stacked pancakes of the floors, with snakes of pneumatic hose trailing behind. They were followed by masked men with oxyacetylene torches and motorized saws. Swinging above them was the crane's writhing cable. The hammering, growling and howling, the clatter of falling rubble, the momentous gonging as sections of floor were dropped into the tippers, kept the curious crowds at bay. Only a few TV crews and photojournalists remained, with their cameras trained on the destruction in the hope of zooming in on a crushed body, a bloodied hand, a spike of bone.

Another helicopter stuttered overhead and wheeled away to fly over the nearby Andalucían Parliament. As he trotted down Calle Los Romeros, Falcón called Ramírez to get the name of the worshipper mentioned by Sr Harrouch, who used the mosque in the mornings. He was called Majid Merizak. Ramírez offered to join him but Falcón preferred to be alone for this one.

The reason that Majid Merizak was not one of the casualties in the mosque was that he was ill in bed. He was a widower who was looked after by one of his daughters. She hadn't been able to prevent her father from heading down the stairs to find out what had happened; only his partial collapse had done that. Now he was in a chair, head thrown back, wild-eyed and panting, with the television on full blast because he was nearly deaf.

The apartment stank of vomit and diarrhoea. He'd been up most of the night and was still weak. The daughter turned off the television and forced her father to wear his hearing aid. She told Falcón that her father's Spanish was poor and Falcón said that they could conduct the interview in Arabic. She explained this to her father, who looked confused and irritable, with too much happening around him. Once his daughter had checked that the hearing aid was functioning properly and had left the room, Majid Merizak sharpened up.

'You speak Arabic?' he asked.

'I'm still learning. Part of my family is Moroccan.'

He nodded and drank tea through Falcón's introduction and visibly relaxed on hearing Falcón's rough Arabic. It had been the right thing to do. Merizak was far less wary than Harrouch had been.

Falcón warmed him up with questions about when he attended the mosque – which was every morning, without fail, and he stayed there until the early afternoon. Then he asked about strangers.

'Last week?' asked Merizak, and Falcón nodded. 'Two young men came in on Tuesday morning, close to midday, and two older men came in on Friday morning at ten o'clock. That's all.'

'And you'd never seen them before?'

'No, but I did see them again yesterday.'

'Who?'

'The two young men who'd come in last Tuesday.'

Merizak's description fitted that of Hammad and Saoudi.

'And what did they do last Tuesday?'

'They went into the Imam's room and talked with him until about one thirty.'

'And what about yesterday morning?'

'They brought in two heavy sacks. It took two of them to carry one sack.'

'What time was this?'

'About ten thirty. The same time that the electricians arrived,' said Merizak. 'Yes, of course, there were the electricians, as well. I'd never seen them before, either.'

'Where did the two young men put these sacks?'

'In the storeroom next to the Imam's office.'

'Do you know what was in the sacks?'

'Couscous. That's what it said on the side.'

'Has anyone made a delivery like that before?'

'Not in those quantities. People have brought in bags of food to give to the Imam . . . you know, it's part of our duty to give to those less fortunate than ourselves.'

'When did they leave?'

'They stayed about an hour.'

'What about the men who came in on Friday?'

'They were inspectors from the council. They went all over the mosque. They discussed things with the Imam and then they left.'

'What about the power cut?'

'That was on Saturday night. I wasn't there. The

Imam was on his own. He said that there was a big bang and the lights went out. That's what he told us the following morning, when we had to pray in the dark.'

'And the electricians came in on Monday to fix it?'

'A man came on his own at eight thirty. Then three other men came two hours later to do the work.'

'Were they Spanish?'

'They were speaking Spanish.'

'What did they do?'

'The fuse box was burned out, so they put in a new one. Then they put in a power socket in the storeroom.'

'What sort of work was that?'

'They cut a channel in the brickwork from a socket in the Imam's office, through the wall and into the storeroom. They put in some grey flexible tubing, fed in the wire and then cemented it all up.'

Merizak had seen the blue transit van, which he described as battered, but he hadn't seen any markings or the registration number.

'How did the Imam pay for the work?'

'Cash.'

'Do you know where he got the phone number of this company?'

'No.'

'Would you recognize the electricians, council inspectors and two young men if you saw them again?'

'Yes, but I can't describe them to you very well.'

'You've been listening to the news?'

'They don't know what they're talking about,' said Merizak. 'It makes me very angry. A bomb explodes and it is automatically Islamic militants.'

'Have you ever heard of Los Mártires Islámicos para la Liberación de Andalucía?'

'The first time was on the news today. It's an invention of the media to discredit Islam.'

'Have you ever heard of the Imam preaching militant ideology in the mosque?'

'Quite the opposite.'

'I'm told that the Imam was a very capable linguist.'

'He learnt Spanish very quickly. They said his apartment was full of French and English books. He spoke German, too. He spoke on the telephone using languages I'd never heard before. He told me that one of them was Turkish. Some people came here in February and stayed with him for a week and that was another strange language. Somebody said it was Pashto, and that the men were from Afghanistan.'

14

The offices of the *ABC* newspaper, a glass cylinder on the Isla de la Cartuja, had been as close to bedlam as a hysterical business like journalism could get. Angel Zarrías watched from the edge of the newsroom as journalists roared down telephones, bawled at assistants and harangued each other.

Through the flickering computer screens, the phone lines stretched to snapping point and the triangles formed by hands slapped to foreheads, Angel was watching the open door of the editor's office. He was biding his time. This was the newshounds' moment. It was their job to find the stories, which the editor would knit together to construct the right image and tone, for the new history of a city in crisis.

On the way from Manuela's apartment to the *ABC* offices he'd asked the taxi to drop him off in a street near the Maestranza bullring where his friend Eduardo Rivero lived and which also housed the headquarters of his political party: Fuerza Andalucía. He'd been dining with Eduardo Rivero and the new sponsors of Fuerza Andalucía last night. A momentous decision had been made, which he hadn't been able to share with Manuela until it became official today. He had also not been able to tell her that he was now going to be working more for Fuerza Andalucía than the *ABC*. He had a lot more important things on his mind than grumbling about same-sex marriages in his daily political column.

Rivero's impressive house bore all the hallmarks of his traditional upbringing and thinking. Its façade was painted to a deep terracotta finish, the window surrounds were picked out in ochre and all caged in magnificent wrought-iron grilles. The main door was three metres high, built out of oak, varnished to the colour of chestnuts and studded with brass medallions. It opened on to a huge marble-flagged patio, in which Rivero had departed briefly from tradition by planting two squares of box hedge. In the centre of each was a statue; to the left was Apollo and to the right Dionysus, and in between was the massive bowl of a white marble fountain, whose restrained trickles of water held the house, despite these pagan idols, in a state of religious obeisance.

The front of the house was the party headquarters, with the administration below and the policy-making and political discussions going on above. Angel took the stairs just inside the main door, which led up to Rivero's office. They were waiting for him; Rivero and his second-in-command, the much younger Jesús Alarcón.

Unusually, he and Rivero were sitting together in the middle of the room, with the boss's wood and leather armchair empty behind his colossal English oak desk. They all shook hands. Rivero, the same age as Angel, seemed remarkably relaxed. He wasn't even wearing a tie, his jacket was hanging off the back of his chair. He was smiling beneath an ebullient white moustache. He did not look as if scandal had come anywhere near him.

'Like any good journalist, Angel, you've arrived at the crucial moment,' said Rivero. 'A decision has been made.'

'I don't believe it,' said Angel.

'Well, you'll have to believe it, because it's true,' said Rivero. 'I'd like you to meet the new leader of Fuerza Andalucía, Jesús Alarcón. Effective as from five minutes ago.'

'I think that's a bold and brilliant decision,' said Angel, shaking them both by the hand and embracing them. 'And one you've been keeping very quiet.'

'The committee voted on it last night before we met for dinner,' said Rivero. 'I didn't want to break the news until I had asked Jesús and he'd accepted. Something was going to have to happen before the 2007 campaign and, with this morning's explosion, that campaign will be starting today – and what better way to kick it off than with a new leader?'

Alarcón's expression was a mask of seriousness that bore all the weight and lines of the gravity that the situation demanded, but it could not hide what came shining out from within. His grey suit, dark tie and white shirt could not contain his sense of achievement. He was the schoolboy at the prize-giving, who'd already been told that he had won the top award.

Angel Zarrías had known Jesús Alarcón since the year 2000, when he'd been introduced to him by his old friend, Lucrecio Arenas the Chief Executive Officer of the Banco Omni in Madrid. In the last six years Angel had drawn Jesús into Eduardo Rivero's orbit and gradually eased him into positions of greater importance within the party. Angel had never had any doubt about Alarcón's brains, his political commitment or astuteness, but, as an old PR man, he had been worried by his lack of charisma. But the final wresting of the leadership from Rivero's trembling clutches had wrought an extraordinary change in the younger man. Physically he was the same, but his confidence had become dazzlingly palpable. Angel couldn't help himself. He embraced Jesús once again as the new leader of Fuerza Andalucía.

'As you know,' said Rivero, 'in the last three elections there has been steady growth in our share of the vote, but it has only grown to a maximum of 4.2 per cent and that is not enough for us to be the chosen partner of the Partido Popular. We need a new kind of energy at the top.'

'I have the business experience,' said Alarcón, breaking in with his new-found confidence, 'to raise our funding to unprecedented levels, but this is of limited significance in a torpid political atmosphere. What this morning's event has given us is a unique opportunity to focus voters' minds on the real and perceivable threat of radical Islam. It gives our immigration policy new bite where before, even after 11th March, it was dismissed as extreme and out of step with the ways in which contemporary societies were developing. If we spend the next eight months getting that message across to the population of Andalucía then we stand a chance of a substantial increase in our share of the vote, come 2007. So we have the right ideology for the time, and I can raise the money to make it heard across the region.'

'We don't think that it's a coincidence that the first call after the explosion in El Cerezo this morning should be from you, Angel,' said Rivero. 'You, more than anybody else, know what would make an enormous impression on the population of Andalucía tomorrow morning.'

Angel sat back in his chair, ran his fingers through his hair and hissed air out from between his clenched teeth. He knew what Rivero wanted and it was a tall order under the circumstances.

'Just think of the impact it would have,' said Rivero, nodding at Jesús, 'his face, his profile and his ideas in the pages of *ABC Sevilla* on the day after such a catastrophe as this. We would tread Izquierda Unida into the dust and make the Partido Andalucista writhe in their beds at night.'

'Are you ready for what I can do for you?' asked Angel.

'I'm more prepared for it than at any time in my life,' said Alarcón, and handed him his CV.

Angel had sat in the back of the cab on the way to the *ABC* offices, leafing through Alarcón's CV. Jesús Alarcón was born in Cordoba in 1965. He'd been accepted at Madrid University at the age of seventeen to study philosophy, political history and economics. As a staunch Catholic he despised the atheistic creed of communism and believed that the best way to break one's enemy was to know them. He went to Berlin University to study Russian and Russian political history. He was there – and a photograph existed to support this – when the Wall came down in 1989. It wasn't supposed to have happened like that and the crucial event had left him bereft of a cause.

At the same time his father's business collapsed and

he died soon after. His mother followed her husband into the grave six months later and Jesús applied to INSEAD in Paris to do an MBA. By Christmas 1991 he was working for McKinsey's in Boston, and in the following four years became one of their analysts and consultants in Central and South America. In 1995 he moved to Lehman Brothers, to join their mergers and acquisitions team. There he changed his sphere of operations to the European Union and built up a powerful list of investors looking to buy into the booming Spanish economy. In 1997 his life changed again when he met a beautiful Sevillana called Mónica Abellón, whose father had been one of Jesús's leading clients. Mónica's father effected an introduction to Lucrecio Arenas, who head-hunted him for the secretive Banco Omni and he moved to Madrid, where Mónica was working as a model.

It was in the year 2000 that Angel, totally fed up with the Partido Popular, had taken on some PR work for Banco Omni clients. Lucrecio Arenas, convinced that he'd discovered a future leader of Spain in Jesús Alarcón, was eager for his new find to cut his teeth in regional politics, and had enlisted Angel's help. As soon as Angel introduced Alarcón to Eduardo Rivero and the other Fuerza Andalucía committee members, they welcomed him into the fold, recognizing one of their own. Jesús Alarcón was a traditionalist, a practising Catholic, a man who loathed communism and socialism, a believer in the power of business to do good in society and also a lover of the bulls. He was twenty years younger than any of them. He was good looking, if a little on the dull side, but he made up for it by having the beautiful Mónica Abellón as his wife, and two gorgeous children.

In the *ABC* offices Angel went to work on the dossier and archives. In an hour he'd put together a page, the editor was never going to look at more than that. The headline: THIS MAN HAS ANSWERS. The main shot was part of a photograph he'd found of Jesús in a business magazine about Spain's future. Jesús was supposedly looking up to a sun, which was probably a photographer's lighting umbrella, and his face was shining with hope and belief in the future. He also had shots of Jesús with the stunning Mónica, and the couple with their children. There was a sub headline, which said: *The New Leader of Fuerza Andalucía Believes in Our Future.* The writing was in note form and described not just the radical immigration policy of Fuerza Andalucía, but also vital economic and agrarian reforms that were necessary to make Andalucía a force in the future. It included Jesús's employment profile, which showed that he was economically 'sensible', internationally connected and had the contacts in industry to make his ideas work.

There was a lull in activity just before lunch at around two o'clock. The traffic into the editor's office had calmed. Angel made his move.

'We're probably going to have to cut your column for at least the next few days,' said the editor when he saw Angel crossing his threshold.

'Of course,' said Angel. 'Nobody wants political gossip at a time like this.'

'What do you want with me, then?' said the editor, interested now he knew that Angel hadn't come for a fight.

'Most of the stuff in tomorrow's newspaper is going to be hard news and a lot of it will be heart-rending, with reports on the destruction of the pre-school and the dead children. The only positive stories will be about the excellence of the emergency services, and I've heard that there's a survivor. You'll be writing a leader that captures the mood of the city, that reacts to the receipt of Abdullah Azzam's text, and that declares that we might not have moved so far forward since 11th March as everybody would like to think.'

'Well, Angel, now you've told me my job,' said the editor, 'you can get on with telling me what you're proposing.'

'A vision of hope,' he said, handing over the page he'd just created. 'In this time of crisis there's a young, energetic, capable man in the wings, who could make Andalucía a safe and prosperous place to live.'

The editor scanned the page, took it all in, nodded and grunted.

'So the rumours about Eduardo Rivero *are* true.'

'I'm not sure what you're referring to.'

'Come off it, Angel,' said the editor, flinging out a dismissive fist. 'He was caught with his pants down.'

'I don't think there's any truth in that.'

'With an under-age girl. There was talk of a DVD.'

'Nobody's seen it.'

'The rumblings have been very loud, and now this –' said the editor, waving the page in the air. 'If it wasn't for the bomb, I'd have someone digging in the dirt after your old friend.'

'Look, this has been in the pipeline for a long time,' said Angel. 'With this bomb going off he just feels that it's time to stand down and let somebody younger take the party to the next stage. He's going to be seventy at the end of this year.'

'So we have the first political casualty of the bomb.'

'That's not how we should be thinking about it,' said Angel. 'It's precipitated change and it's saying that change is what we have to do if we want to survive this challenge to our liberty.'

'You're serious, Angel. What's happened to the great deflator? The man with the sharpened nib who pops those hot-air egos?'

'Perhaps my cynicism is another casualty of the bomb.'

'Well, you're always complaining that nothing happens,' said the editor, 'and now . . . you believe in this guy and yet you've barely written a word about him before.'

'As you've just pointed out, my column was primarily for puncturing egos,' said Angel. 'Jesús Alarcón hasn't had time to develop an ego that needs to be punctured. He's quietly taken Fuerza Andalucía from being an organization with a small debt to one with regular contributions from members and businesses. He's done amazing, if uncharismatic, work.'

'So what makes you think he's got the personality for it?'

'I saw him this morning,' said Angel. 'He's learnt a lot . . .'

'But can you *learn* charisma?'

'Charisma is just an intense form of self-belief,' said Angel. 'Jesús Alarcón has always been confident. He's ambitious. He's dealt with serious personal setbacks, which, to me, are a far more powerful measure of the man than his ability to broker international finance deals. He has the inner steel and common sense that our last prime minister had. You know politics. It's like boxing. It's all very well to have the fast hands and fancy footwork, but even the greatest fighters get hit very hard and if you can't absorb punishment you're finished. Jesús Alarcón has all those qualities and, after the conferring of the leadership, I can now see emerging that indefinable quality that will make people want to follow him.'

'All right,' said the editor, thinking positively about it. 'A new face for a new era. Write me a profile. And, by the way, I agree with you about charisma, it *is* an intense form of self-belief. But there's something both blinding *and* blind about it, too. Its closest friend can quite quickly become corruption – the belief that you can do anything with impunity. I hope Jesús Alarcón does not have the makings of a tragic figure.'

'He's not a hollow man,' said Angel. 'He's suffered and come through it.'

'Get him to remember that suffering,' said the editor. 'Every politician should have the words of the president of the Terrorists' Victims' Association, Pilar Manjón, ringing in their ears: "They only think of themselves."'

The Madrid police and forensics had been working hard in the apartment used by Djamel Hammad and Smail Saoudi. Taped to the underside of a gas bottle they'd found a selection of stolen and forged IDs and passports, with pictures of the two men whose descriptions fitted those given by Trabelsi Amar and the Seville homicide squad. They'd also discovered € 5,875 in small-denomination notes in three separate packages hidden around the apartment. DNA was currently being generated from hairs, bristles and pubic hairs found in the

200

bathroom. An empty pad on the kitchen table had revealed indentations, which proved to be complicated directions to a property southwest of Madrid, not far from a village called Valmojado. The isolated house near the Río Guadarrama was found to be empty, with no evidence of recent habitation. The police concluded that it was a staging post – a place to pick up and leave material – and nothing more. The property had been rented in the name of a Spaniard, whose ID was false. The owners had been paid six months in advance, which had made them reluctant to ask too many questions. The forensics were still conducting their search of the premises, but so far not a trace of explosive had been found. The Guardia Civil had questioned a number of locals, including shepherds, and reckoned that in the four months it had been rented it had been visited by a white van five times. Three of those visits corresponded roughly to the times Trabelsi Amar had lent the Peugeot Partner to Hammad and Saoudi.

There was a complication with this scenario, which was that the directions to the isolated house found in the Madrid apartment were freshly written in Hammad's handwriting, which would imply that their visit on Sunday at around midday was their first. This in turn implied that the other two times they'd borrowed Trabelsi Amar's van they'd lent it to others who had gone to the farmhouse. A clearer indication that the isolated farmhouse was being visited by people other than Hammad and Saoudi came from eyewitness reports that as many as six different people, including one woman, had been seen going there. This information had an adrenalizing effect on the CGI in Madrid, who concluded that Hammad and Saoudi were acting within a much larger network than at first thought. They contacted all the major intelligence agencies but none of them had picked up any 'chatter' about a planned attack in Spain. The fear now was that Hammad and Saoudi's logistical work was part of a wider effort.

The CGI, with the help of the Guardia Civil, were now trying to find Hammad and Saoudi's route from Madrid to the isolated house near Valmojado and then down to Seville. They wanted to know if they had made any other stopovers – anonymous-looking meetings in roadside bars, other visits to isolated houses or, worse, other deliveries to, for instance, a location in another major Andalucían city.

That was the primary content of a seven-page report, drafted by several senior officers of the counterterrorism unit and sent by the Madrid CGI to Comisario Elvira in the damaged pre-school in Seville. There was a conclusion attached, which had been written by the Director of the CNI and had also reached the hands of Prime Minister Zapatero:

> On the basis of our own findings and the reports received so far from the offices of the CGI and, taken in conjunction with the preliminary reports from the bomb squad and the police on the ground at the site of the disaster, we can only conclude, at this point, that we have come across an Islamic terrorist network who were planning an attack, or, more likely, a series of attacks, with the intention of destabilizing the political and social fabric of the region of Andalucía. Whilst the investigating bodies have so far uncovered some anomalies to the usual modus operandi of radical Islamic groups, they

have not brought to our attention any suspicious activity,
or even stated intention, of any other group that might
want to inflict damage on the Muslim population of
Andalucía. We therefore recommend that the govern-
ment take the necessary steps to protect all major cities
in the region.

The noise of demolition work reasserted itself in the room after Comisario Elvira finished the reading of the report. Inspector Jefe Falcón and Juez Calderón were sitting on small children's desks, arms folded, ankles crossed and staring into the ground, which had now been swept clear of glass. Plastic sheeting, which had been stretched across the empty window frames, revealed an indistinct outside world that ballooned and lurched with the hot breeze, blowing from the south.

'They seem to have made up their minds, don't they?' said Calderón. 'Having told us not to disappear exclusively down one path, that's just what they've done themselves. There's no mention of the VOMIT website or of any other anti-Muslim groups.'

'Given all the stuff they've just found in the Madrid apartment of Hammad and Saoudi, and the hexogen deposit in the rear of the Peugeot Partner and the Islamic paraphernalia in the front,' said Elvira, 'who could blame them?'

'It doesn't look good for the Islamic radicals at the moment,' said Falcón. 'But the bomb squad haven't got to the epicentre of the explosion yet. There's still vital forensic information to come. I've also spoken to the forensics going over the Peugeot Partner and so far all they've come up with is that a new tyre had been fitted to the rear driver's side and the spare had a puncture.

'What they've found in the Madrid apartment and the existence of the isolated house could be interpreted as terrorist activity, or illegal immigrant activity. We've been told that Hammad and Saoudi have a track record of logistical involvement, but what does that mean? If they'd been caught with something, then we'd know about it. If they've been named by others, that's questionable information.'

'My reading of this document,' said Elvira, flapping the paper derisively in front of him, 'is that it's something that has been drafted for the politicians, so that they can appear knowledgeable and decisive on a day of crisis. The CNI and CGI have stuck to the known facts. They've mentioned "anomalies" but have given no detail. VOMIT and other groups aren't mentioned because there's nothing to support their involvement. The MILA doesn't appear either, despite its mention on the news. It's because they've got no intelligence to offer on any of them.'

'Are we allowed to talk about the CGI?' said Falcón, purposely disingenuous.

Calderón's secrecy radar was on to it in a flash. Elvira threw up his hands.

'Needless to say, this can't go out of this room,' said Elvira, 'but seeing as you're the instructing judge controlling this investigation you should know that there have been some concerns about the reliability of the Seville branch of the CGI. A decision from above has not yet been taken to allow them to fully enter the battle. Their agents have been in touch with their informer network and have drafted reports, but we haven't seen anything yet. They've been denied access to our reports and they know nothing about certain pieces of evidence, such as the heavily annotated copy of the Koran, which, as far as I know, has been kept out of the news.'

'That's a big blow to the investigation,' said Calderón. 'Shouldn't we have heard about this before now?'

'I don't have clearance to tell either of you,' said Elvira.

'So what is it about this heavily annotated copy of the Koran that's so important?' asked Calderón.

'I don't know, but it's received a very high level of interest from the CNI,' said Elvira. 'Anyway, that doesn't concern us right now. When was the last time you heard from your squad?'

'Recently enough to be able to say that we've got a pretty clear picture of what happened here in the last forty-eight hours, some of which is connected to occurrences in the week before the explosion.'

Falcón now had at least two witnesses to each of the significant events that preceded the blast. Hammad and Saoudi had first been seen at the mosque on Tuesday 30th May at 12.00. They arrived on foot and stayed talking to the Imam until 1.30 p.m. The two other events of that week were the visit from council inspectors at 10 a.m. on Friday 2nd June and a power cut some time on Saturday 3rd June at night, when the Imam had been in the mosque alone.

This led to an electrician turning up at 8.30 a.m. on Monday 5th June to assess the damage and the work involved. He returned with two labourers at 10.30 a.m. to repair the blown fuse box and also install a power socket in the storeroom next to the Imam's office.

The second visit from the electrician coincided with Hammad and Saoudi's arrival in the Peugeot Partner and the unloading of two large polypropylene sacks, which were believed to contain couscous. They stayed about an hour. The electricians left just before lunch at about 2.30 p.m. Hammad and Saoudi returned at 5.45 p.m. with four heavy cardboard boxes believed to contain sugar and some carrier bags of mint, all of which went into the storeroom. They were still there at 7 p.m. and, so far, nobody had seen them leave the premises.

'And what are your areas of concern in all that?'

'We have witnesses to the arrivals and departures of all these people,' said Falcón. 'But we haven't been able to make contact with the electrician. In order to get this done as quickly as possible I've asked my squad, who are already overloaded with interview work, to co-ordinate with local police and get them to visit every electrician's outlet or workshop within a square kilometre of the explosion. So far we've come up with nothing. All we know is that three men arrived in a blue transit van with no markings and we have no witnesses for the registration number.'

'Do you want the media to make an announcement?' asked Elvira.

'Not yet. I want to do more footwork on this.'

'What else?'

'I have other members of my squad tied up interviewing the Informáticalidad sales reps. None of them has come back to me with anything significant, but I have yet to talk to them and find out what the story was there.'

'Is that it?'

'My greatest concern at the moment, apart from the

undiscovered electrician, is that the council have no record of sending any inspectors to the mosque, or any other part of this building, or even this barrio, on Friday 2nd June, or any day, for that matter, in the last three months.'

15

Before the three men left the bombsite for the night, Calderón gave an update on the deaths and injuries. Four children had died of head wounds and internal bleeding in the pre-school. Seven children had been seriously wounded – ranging from the loss of a leg below the knee to severe facial lacerations. Eighteen children had been lightly wounded, mainly cut by flying glass. Two men and a woman who had been passing by the building on Calle Los Romeros had been killed, either by flying debris or falling masonry. An elderly woman had died of a heart attack in an apartment across the road. There were thirty-two seriously injured people, who had been either inside, or around, buildings close to the stricken block and there were three hundred and forty-three lightly injured. From the rubble they had so far removed two men and two women who were dead and young Lourdes Alanis, who had survived. The list of missing in the mosque, including the Imam, numbered thirteen. Apart from them this gave a total so far of twelve dead, thirty-nine seriously injured and three hundred and sixty-one lightly injured.

The demolition crews were now removing the remaining slabs of concrete from what had been the fifth floor. The whole area was under floodlights as they prepared to work all night. An air-conditioned tent had been erected on some wasteground between the pre-school and another block of apartments to handle forensic evidence. Another tent was being erected to deal with the bodies and body parts, which would eventually be coming out of the crushed mosque. The judges, homicide squad, forensics and emergency services had worked out a duty roster, so that there would be someone on site all night from each group.

It was still light and very warm as Elvira, Falcón and Calderón left the pre-school just before 8 p.m. A group of people had gathered in a corner of the playground. Hundreds of candles flickered on the ground amidst bouquets of flowers. Banners and placards had been pinned up on the chain-link fencing – *No más muertes. Paz. Sólo los inocentes han caido. Por el derecho de vivir sin violencia* – No more death. Peace. Only the innocents have fallen. For the right to live without violence. But the largest banner of all was written in red against a white background – *ODIO ETERNO AL TERRORISMO* – Eternal Hate to Terrorism. In the bottom right-hand corner was written VOMIT. Falcón asked if anybody had seen the person who had unfurled this banner, but nobody had. It was this banner which had drawn people to that part of the playground and so it had become a natural place for the locals to pay tribute to the fallen.

They stood in the violet light of a sun that was beginning to set on this catastrophic day and, with the

209

machinery inexorably clawing away at the piled rubble, their murmured prayers, guttering candles and the already wilting flowers were both pathetic and touching, as pitiful and moving as the futile deaths of all humans in the vast grotesqueness of war. As the lawmen backed away from the shrine, Elvira's mobile rang. He took the call and handed it to Falcón. It was Juan from the CNI, saying that they had to meet tonight. Falcón said he would be home in an hour.

The hospital was calm after the frenetic activity of the day. In the emergency room they were still picking glass out of people's faces and suturing lacerations. There were patients in the waiting room, but there was no longer the horror of the triage nurse wading through the victims, skidding on blood, looking into the wide, dark eyes of the injured, silently pleading. Falcón showed his police ID and asked for Lourdes Alanis, who was in the intensive care unit on the first floor.

Through the glass panels of the intensive care unit Fernando was visible at his daughter's bedside, holding her hand. She was hooked up to machines but seemed to be breathing on her own. The doctor in the ICU said she was making good progress. She had sustained a broken arm and a crushed leg, but no spinal injuries. Their main concern had been her head injuries. She was still in a coma, but a scan had revealed no evidence of brain damage or haemorrhaging. As they talked, Fernando left the ICU to go to the toilet. Falcón gave him a few minutes and went in after him. He was washing his hands and face.

'Who are you?' he asked, looking at Falcón via the mirror, suspicious, knowing he wasn't a doctor.

'We met earlier today by your apartment block. My name is Javier Falcón. I'm the Inspector Jefe of the homicide squad.'

Fernando frowned, shook his head; he didn't remember.

'Does this mean that you've caught the people who destroyed my family?'

'No, we're still working on that.'

'You won't have to look very far. That rat hole is crawling with them.'

'With who?'

'Fucking Moroccans,' he said. 'Those fucking bastards. We've been looking at them all this time, ever since 11th March, and we've been thinking . . . when's the next time going to be. We always knew that there was going to be a next time.'

'Who is "we"?'

'Alright, me. That's what *I've* been thinking,' said Fernando. 'But I know I'm not alone.'

'I didn't think the relations between the communities were so bad,' said Falcón.

'That's because you don't live in "the communities",' said Fernando. 'I've seen the news, full of nice, comfortable people telling you that everything is all right, that Muslims and Catholics are communicating, that there's some kind of "healing process" going on. I can tell you, it's all bullshit. We live in a state of suspicion and fear.'

'Even though you know that very few members of the Muslim population are terrorists?'

'That's what we're told, but we don't *know* it,' said Fernando. 'And what's more, we have no idea who *they* are. They could be standing next to me in the bar, drinking beer and eating *jamón*. Yes, you see, some of

211

them even do that. Eat pig and drink alcohol. But it seems that they're just as likely to blow themselves up as the one who spends his life with his nose to the floor in the mosque.'

'I didn't come here to make you angry,' said Falcón. 'You've got enough to think about without that.'

'You didn't *make* me angry. I *am* angry. I've *been* angry a long time. Two years and three months I've been angry,' said Fernando. 'Gloria, my wife . . .'

He stopped. His face came apart. His mouth thickened with saliva. He had to support himself against the basin as the physical pain worked its way through. It took some minutes for him to pull himself together.

'Gloria was a good person. She believed in the good that exists in everyone. But her belief didn't protect her, it didn't protect our son. The people she spoke up for killed her, in the same way that they killed the ones they hate, and who hate them. Anyway, that's enough. I must get back to my daughter. I know you didn't have to come and find me here. You've got a lot on your plate. So I thank you for that . . . for your concern. And I wish you well in your investigation. I hope you find the killers before I do.'

'I want you to call me,' said Falcón, giving him his card, 'at any time, day or night, for whatever reason. If you're angry, depressed, violent, lonely or even hungry, I want you to call me.'

'I didn't think you people were supposed to get personally involved.'

'I also want you to tell me if you're ever contacted by a group who call themselves VOMIT, so it's important on two levels that we keep in touch.'

They left the toilet and shook hands outside, where,

on the other side of the glass, his daughter's life was readable in green on the screens. Fernando hesitated as he leaned against the door.

'Only one politician spoke to me today,' he said. 'I saw them all parading themselves before the cameras with the victims and their families. This was while they were operating on Lourdes' skull, so I had time to look at their ridiculous antics. Only one person found me.'

'Who was that?'

'Jesús Alarcón,' said Fernando. 'I'd never heard of him before. He's the new leader of Fuerza Andalucía.'

'What did he say to you?'

'He didn't say anything. He listened – and there wasn't a camera in sight.'

The sky darkened to purple over the old city like the discoloration around a recent wound that had begun to hurt in earnest. Falcón drove on automatic, his mind buried deep in intractable problems: a bomb explodes, killing, maiming and destroying. What is left after the dust clears and the bodies are taken away is a horrendous social and political confusion, where emotions rise to the surface and, like wind on the susceptible grass of the plain, influence can blow people's minds this way and that, turn them from beer-sippers into chest-thumpers.

The three CNI men were waiting for him outside his house on Calle Bailén. He parked his car in front of the oak doors. They all shook hands and followed him through to the patio, which was looking a little dishevelled these days. Encarnación, his housekeeper, wasn't as capable as she used to be and Falcón didn't have the money for the renovation required. And

213

anyway, he'd grown to enjoy living in the encroaching shabbiness of his surroundings.

He dragged some chairs out around a marble-topped table on the patio and left the CNI men to listen to the water trickling in the fountain. He came back with cold beers, olives, capers, pickled garlic, crisps, bread, cheese and *jamón*. They ate and drank and talked about Spain's chances in the World Cup in Germany; always the same – a team full of genius and promise, which was never fulfilled.

'Do you have any idea why we want to talk to you?' asked Pablo, who was more relaxed now, less intensely observant.

'Something to do with my Moroccan connections, so I was told.'

'You're a very interesting man to us,' said Pablo. 'We don't want to hide the fact that we've been looking at you for some time now.'

'I'm not sure that I've got the right mentality for secret work any more. If you'd asked me five years ago, then you might have found the ideal candidate . . .'

'Who is the ideal candidate?' asked Juan.

'Someone who is already hiding a great deal from the world, from his family, from his wife, and from himself. A few state secrets on top wouldn't be such a burden.'

'We don't want you to be a spy,' said Juan.

'Do you want me to deceive?'

'No, we think deceiving would be a very bad idea under the circumstances.'

'You'll understand better what we want by answering a few questions,' said Pablo, wresting the interview back from his boss.

214

'Don't make them too difficult,' said Falcón. 'I've had a long day.'

'Tell us how you came to meet Yacoub Diouri.'

'That could take some time,' said Falcón.

'We're not in any hurry,' said Pablo.

And, as if at some prearranged signal, Juan and Gregorio sat back, took out cigarette packs and lit up. It was one of those occasions after a long day, with a little beer and food inside him, that made Falcón wish he was still a smoker.

'I think you probably know that just over five years ago, on 12th April 2001, I ran a murder investigation into the brutal killing of an entrepreneur turned restaurateur called Raúl Jiménez.'

'You've got a policeman's memory for dates,' said Juan.

'You'll find that date written in scar tissue on my heart when I'm dead,' said Falcón. 'It's got nothing to do with being a policeman.'

'It had a big impact on your life?' said Pablo.

Falcón took another fortifying gulp of Cruzcampo.

'The whole of Spain knows this story. It was all over the newspapers for weeks,' said Falcón, a little irritated with the knowingness with which the questions had started coming at him.

'We weren't in Spain at the time,' said Juan. 'We've read the files, but it's not the same as hearing it for real.'

'My investigation into Raúl Jiménez's past showed that he'd known my father, the artist Francisco Falcón. They'd started a smuggling business together in Tangier during and after the Second World War. It meant they could establish themselves and start families and

215

Francisco Falcón could begin the process of turning himself into an artist.'

'And what about Raúl Jiménez?' said Pablo. 'Didn't he meet his wife when she was very young?'

'Raúl Jiménez had an unhealthy obsession with young girls,' said Falcón, taking a deep breath, knowing what they were after. 'It wasn't *so* unusual in those days in Tangier or Andalucía for a girl to get married at thirteen, but in fact her parents made Raúl wait until she was seventeen. They had a couple of children, but they were difficult births and the doctor recommended that his wife didn't have any more.

'In the run-up to Moroccan independence in the 1950s, Raúl became involved with a businessman called Abdullah Diouri who had a young daughter. Raúl had sex with this girl and, I think, even got her pregnant. This would not have been a problem had he done the honourable thing and married the girl. In Muslim society he would have just taken a second wife and that would have been the end of it. As a Catholic, it was impossible. To complicate matters further, despite doctor's orders, his wife became pregnant with their third child.

'In the end Raúl took the coward's way out and fled with his family. Abdullah Diouri was incensed when he discovered this and wrote a letter to Francisco Falcón in which he told him of Raúl's betrayal and expressed his determination to be avenged, which he achieved five years later.

'The third child, a boy called Arturo, was kidnapped on his way back from school in southern Spain. Raúl Jiménez's way of dealing with this terrible loss was to deny the boy's existence. It devastated the family. His wife committed suicide and the children were damaged, one of them beyond repair.'

'Was it that sad story that made you decide to try to find Arturo thirty-seven years after he had disappeared?' asked Pablo.

'As you know, I met Raúl's second wife, Consuelo, while investigating his murder. About a year later we started a relationship and during that time we revealed to each other that the one thing that still haunted us about her husband's murder case, and all that surfaced with it, was the disappearance of Arturo. There was still a part of us that imagined the eternally lost six-year-old boy.'

'That was in July 2002,' said Pablo. 'When did you start looking for Arturo?'

'In September of that year,' said Falcón. 'Neither of us could believe that Abdullah Diouri would have killed the child. We thought he would have drawn him into his family in some way.'

'And what was driving you?' asked Juan. 'The lost boy . . . or something else?'

'I knew very well I was looking for a forty-three-year-old man.'

'Had something happened to your relationship with Consuelo Jiménez in the meantime?' asked Pablo.

'It finished almost as soon as it started, but I'm not going to discuss that with you.'

'Didn't Consuelo Jiménez break off the relationship?' asked Pablo.

'She broke it off,' said Falcón, throwing up his hands, realizing that the whole of the Jefatura knew what had happened. 'She didn't want to get involved.'

'And you were unhappy?'

'I was *very* unhappy about it.'

'So what was your motive in looking for Arturo?' asked Juan.

'Consuelo refused to see me or speak to me. She cut me out of her life.'

'Not unlike what Raúl had tried to do with Arturo,' said Juan.

'If you like.'

Juan took a pickled garlic and bit into it with a light crunch.

'I realized that the only way I'd be able to see her again under the right circumstances, rather than as a mad stalker, was to do something extraordinary. I knew that if I found Arturo she would have to see me again. It was the way we had connected in the first place and I knew it would stir something in her.'

'And did it work?' asked Juan, fascinated by Falcón's torment.

16

A warm breeze made a circuit of the patio and stirred up a large, dead and dried-out plant in a far dark corner of the cloister.

'I think it would be better to approach this chronologically,' said Pablo. 'Why don't you tell us how you found Arturo Jiménez?'

The rustle and rattle of the plant's dead leaves had drawn Falcón's gaze to its desiccated corner. He had to get rid of that plant.

'Because my search for Arturo was motivated by this hope for reconciliation with Consuelo, I imagined it as a sort of quest. It was a little more straightforward than that. I was lucky to have some help,' said Falcón. 'I went to Fès with a member of my new Moroccan family. He found a guide who took us to Abdullah Diouri's house deep in the medina. Apart from a magnificently carved door, the house looked like nothing from the outside. But the door opened into a paradise of patios, pools and miniature gardens, which had been allowed to decay from some greater former glory. There were tiles missing and cracked paving and the latticework

219

around the gallery was broken in places. The servant who let us in told us that Abdullah Diouri had died some twenty years ago but that his memory lived on, as he had been a great and kind man.

'We asked to speak to any of the sons, but he told us that only women lived in this house. The sons had dispersed throughout Morocco and the Middle East. So we asked if one of the women would be willing to speak to us about this delicate matter that had occurred some forty years ago. He took our names and left. He returned after quarter of an hour and told my Moroccan relative to stay at the door while he took me on a long trip through the house. We ended up on the first floor, with a view through some repaired latticework on to a garden below. He left me there and after a while I realized that there was somebody else in the room. A woman dressed in black, her face totally veiled, pointed me to a seat and I told her my story.

'Fortunately I'd talked to my Moroccan family about what I was intending to do, so I knew I had to be very careful about how I related this story. It had to be from the Moroccan perspective.'

'What did that entail?' asked Juan.

'That Raúl Jiménez had to be the villain of the piece and Abdullah Diouri the saviour of the family honour. If I sullied the name of the patriarch in any way, if I made him out to be a criminal, a kidnapper of children, I would get nowhere. It was good advice. The woman listened to me in silence, still as a statue under a black dustsheet. At the end of my story a gloved hand came out of her robe and dropped a card on to a low table between us. Then she got up and left. On the card was printed an address in Rabat with a telephone number and the name Yacoub Diouri. A few minutes later the servant came back and returned me to the front door.'

'Well, not quite the Holy Grail,' said Juan, 'but worthy of something.'

'Moroccans love mystery,' said Falcón. 'Abdullah Diouri was a very devout Muslim and Yacoub later told me that the Fès household was kept in that state in honour of the great man. None of the sons could stand the place, which was why it was so run down, and it had been given over exclusively to the women of the family.'

'So you had an address in Rabat . . .' said Pablo.

'I stayed the night in Meknes and called Yacoub from there. He already knew who I was and what I wanted, and we agreed to meet in his house in Rabat the next day. As you probably know, he lives in a huge modern place, built in the Arab style, in the embassy zone on the edge of the city. There must be two hectares of land with an orange grove, gardens, tennis courts, swimming pools – a small palace. He has liveried servants, rose petals in the fountains – that kind of thing. I was taken to a huge room overlooking one of the swimming pools, with cream leather sofas all around. I was given some mint tea and left to stew for half an hour until Yacoub turned up.'

'Did he look like Raúl?'

'I'd seen shots of Raúl when he was a younger man in Tangier and less battered by life. There were similarities, but Yacoub is a different animal altogether. Raúl's wealth never managed to get rid of the Andaluz peasant, whereas Yacoub is a very sophisticated individual, well-read in Spanish, French and English. He speaks German, too. His business demands it. He makes clothes for all the major manufacturers in Europe. He's got Dior and Adolfo Dominguez on his client list. Yacoub was a cheetah to Raúl's gnarled old lion.'

'So how did that first meeting go?' asked Pablo.

'We hit it off immediately, which doesn't happen to me very often,' said Falcón. 'These days I seem to find it hard to get on with people of my own class and background, while I seem to have a talent for engaging with misfits.'

'Why's that?' asked Juan.

'I suppose living with my own horrors has given me the ability to understand the complexities of others, or, at least, not to take things at face value,' said Falcón. 'Whatever, Yacoub and I became friends in that first meeting, and, although we don't see very much of each other, we still are. In fact, he called me last night to say he wanted to meet in Madrid at the weekend.'

'Did Yacoub know *your* story?'

'He'd read it in the press at the time of the Francisco Falcón scandal. It was big news over there that the famous Falcón nudes were actually painted by the Moroccan artist, Tariq Chefchaouni.'

'I'm surprised some journalist hadn't tried to track him down before,' said Pablo.

'They had,' said Falcón. 'But they didn't get any further than the outside of Abdullah Diouri's house in Fès.'

'You said Yacoub was a misfit,' said Gregorio. 'He doesn't sound like one. Successful businessman, married, two children, devout Muslim. He seems to fit in perfectly.'

'Well, that's how it looks from the outside, but from

the moment I first met him I knew he was restless,'
said Falcón. 'He was happy with where he was and yet
he felt he didn't belong there. He'd been torn away
from his own family and yet Abdullah Diouri had made
him a part of his and given him the family name. His
real father had never come to search for him and yet
he was treated no differently to Diouri's own sons. He
told me once that he didn't just respect his kidnapper,
Abdullah Diouri, he loved him as a father. But despite
this acceptance from his new family, he never lost that
terrible feeling of having been abandoned by his own.
That's what I call a misfit.'

'You say he's married,' said Pablo. 'How many wives
does he have?'

'Just the one.'

'Isn't that unusual for a man such as Yacoub Diouri?'
asked Juan.

'Why don't you just ask your question to my face
instead of wheedling –'

'Because we're interested in the extent of your relationship with Yacoub. If he's told you intimate details
about himself, then that has meaning for us,' said Juan.

'Yacoub Diouri is homosexual,' said Falcón, wearily.
'His marriage is something that is expected of him by
his society. It is part of his duty as a good Muslim to
take a wife and have children, but his sexual interest
is exclusively with men. And before you let your
prurient interest get carried away, I mean men, not
boys.'

'Why do you think that detail should be important
to us?' asked Juan.

'You're spies, and I just wanted you to know that
his homosexuality is not an area of vulnerability.'

'Why are we questioning you about Yacoub Diouri?' asked Juan.

'First *I'd* like to know how Yacoub came to tell you he was homosexual,' said Pablo.

'Sorry to disappoint you, Pablo, but he didn't make a pass at me,' said Falcón. 'How did *you* find out about him?'

'There's a lot of co-operation between the intelligence services these days,' said Juan. 'Prominent, devout and monied Muslims are . . . observed.'

'Yacoub and I were talking about marriage once and I told him that mine hadn't lasted very long, that my wife had left me for a prominent judge,' said Falcón. 'I told him about Consuelo. He told me that his own marriage was just for show and that he was gay and that the fashion industry suited him.'

'Why?'

'Because it was full of attractive men who weren't looking for a permanent relationship which he couldn't offer.'

Silence. Juan let it be known that it was time to move on.

'So what happened after you became friends with Yacoub?' asked Pablo.

'I saw him quite a lot at the beginning, several times over three or four months. I'd started learning Arabic and went down to see my Moroccan family in Tangier whenever I could. Yacoub would invite me over. We talked, he helped me with my Arabic.'

The CNI men drank their beers in unison.

'And what happened with Consuelo?' asked Juan, blowing smoke out into the night air.

'As I explained, I'd already told Yacoub about

224

Consuelo and my interest in her. He was quite happy to come to Seville and try to help me out. He liked the idea of being a go-between.'

'How long was this after you'd split up with Consuelo?'

'Nearly a year.'

'You took your time.'

'You can't rush these things.'

'How did you communicate,' asked Pablo, 'if she wouldn't speak to you?'

'I wrote her a letter and asked her if she'd like to meet Yacoub,' said Falcón. 'She wrote back and said she would very much like to meet him, but it would have to be alone.'

'You never even got to see Consuelo?' said Juan, amazed.

'Yacoub did his best for me. They liked each other. He asked her out to dinner on my behalf. She refused. He offered to play gooseberry. She turned him down. There were no explanations and that was the end of it,' said Falcón. 'Why don't we have another beer and you tell me the purpose of this intrusive and personal examination?'

In the kitchen Falcón caught sight of his transparent reflection in the darkened window. He hadn't revealed himself to that extent since being in the hands of Alicia Aguado more than four years ago. In fact, he hadn't been intimate with anyone other than Yacoub since then. It hadn't exactly been a relief to talk to strangers like that, but it had brought back a powerful resurgence of his feelings for Consuelo. He even saw himself in the reflection of the window unconsciously rubbing the arm that had brushed against her yesterday. He shook his head and opened another litre of beer.

'You're smiling, Javier,' said Juan, as Falcón came back. 'After an ordeal like that, I'm impressed.'

'I'm solitary, but not depressed,' said Falcón.

'That's not bad going for a middle-aged homicide detective,' said Pablo.

'Being a homicide detective isn't such a problem for me. There aren't that many murders in Seville and I crack most of them, so my work with the homicide squad actually gives me the illusion that problems are being resolved. And, as you know, an illusory state can contribute to sensations of well-being,' said Falcón. 'If I were trying to resolve something like global warming, or the oceans' dwindling fish stocks, then I'd probably be in much worse mental shape.'

'What about global terrorism?' asked Pablo. 'How do you think you'd cope with that?'

'That's not *my* job. I investigate the murder of people by terrorists,' said Falcón. 'I realize that it can be compli-cated. But at least we have a chance at resolution and tragedy brings out the best qualities in most people. I wouldn't want your job, which is to *foresee* and prevent terrorist attacks. If you succeed, you live as unsung heroes. If you fail, you live with the death of inno-cents, the scourge of the media and the admonishment of comfortable politicians. So, no thanks – if you were thinking of offering me a job.'

'Not a job exactly,' said Juan. 'We want to know if you'd be prepared to provide a connective piece or two for the intelligence jigsaw?'

'I've told you that I'm not really spy material any more.'

'In the first instance, we'd be asking you to recruit.'

'You want me to recruit Yacoub Diouri as an intelligence source?' asked Falcón.

The CNI men nodded, gulped beer, lit up cigarettes.

'First of all, I can't think what Yacoub could possibly tell you, and secondly, why me?' said Falcón. 'Surely you've got experienced recruiters who do this sort of thing all the time.'

'It's not what he can tell us now, it's what he could tell us if he was to make a certain move,' said Pablo. 'And you're right, we do have experienced people, but none of them have the special relationship that you do.'

'But my "special relationship" is based on friendship, intimacy and trust, and what will happen to that if one day I say: "Yacoub, will you spy for Spain?"'

'Well, it wouldn't be just for Spain,' said Gregorio. 'It would be for humanity as a whole.'

'Oh, would it really, Gregorio?' said Falcón. 'I'll remember to tell him that, when I ask him to deceive his family and friends and give information to someone he's only known for the last four years of his complicated life.'

'We're not pretending it's easy,' said Juan. 'And equally, we're not going to deny the value of such a contact, or that there are moral implications in what we're asking of you.'

'Thank you, that's put my mind at rest, Juan,' said Falcón. 'You said "in the first instance" – does that mean there's a second one as well? If so, you'd better tell me. I might as well try to digest that with the first lump of gristle you've just thrown me.'

The CNI men looked at each other and shrugged.

227

'We've just been told that they're going to release the antiterrorism unit of the Seville CGI into this investigation,' said Juan. 'We think there's a mole leaking information and we want to know who it is and who he's leaking it to. You're going to have to work closely with them. Your insight would be invaluable.'

'I don't know what makes you think I can do this work.'

'You've just scored very high points in your interview,' said Pablo.

'What was my score on moral certitude?'

The CNI men laughed as one. Not that they found it funny, it was just the relief at having got the ugliness over and done with.

'Do I get anything in return for all this?' asked Falcón.

'More money, if that's what you want,' said Juan, puzzled.

'I was thinking less in terms of euros and more along the lines of trust,' said Falcón.

'Like what?'

'You tell me things,' said Falcón. 'I'm not saying yes or no, you understand, but perhaps you could tell me what's so important about this annotated copy of the Koran that we found in the Peugeot Partner . . .'

'That's not going to be possible at this juncture,' said Pablo.

'We're beginning to think that what we've found here in Seville,' said Juan, overriding his junior officer, 'is the edge of a much larger terrorist plan.'

'Larger than the liberation of Andalucía?' asked Falcón.

'We're inclined to think that it's a sign of something

that's gone wrong in a plan that we know little about,'
said Juan. 'What we think we have in our possession,
in the form of this copy of the Koran, is a terrorist
network's codebook.'

17

The restaurant was in the middle of the first service to the early tourists, before the main rush of locals at 10 p.m. Consuelo left her office to keep her second appointment with Alicia Aguado. She had been out only once, to her sister's house for lunch. They had talked exclusively about the bomb until the last minutes of the meal when Consuelo had asked her if she could be at her home in Santa Clara at around 10.30 p.m. Her sister had assumed that there was a problem with the nanny.

'No, no, she'll be there looking after the boys,' said Consuelo. 'It's just that I've been told I need someone who's close to me to be there when I get back.'

'Are you going to the gynaecologist?'

'No. The *psych*ologist.'

'You?' her sister had said, astonished.

'Yes, Ana, your sister, Consuelo, is going to see a shrink,' she said.

'But you're the most sane person I've ever known,' said Ana. 'If you're nuts, then what hope is there for the rest of us?'

'I'm not *nuts*,' she'd said, 'but I could be. I'm on a knife-edge at the moment. This woman I'm going to see will help me, but she says I need support when I get home. You are the support.'

The effect on her sister was shocking, not least because it had been an unsettling realization for both of them, that perhaps they weren't as close as they'd thought.

As she left the safety of her office, Consuelo felt something like panic forming in her stomach and, as if on cue, she remembered Alicia Aguado's words: 'Come straight to me from your work. Don't be distracted.' It started up some confusion in her, a voice asking: Why shouldn't I? And as she fastened her seat belt, her mind swerved away from its earlier objective and she thought about driving past the Plaza del Pumarejo, wondering if *he* would be there. Her heart raced and she hit the horn so hard and long that one of the waiters came running out into the street. She pulled away and drove straight through the Plaza del Pumarejo, eyes fixed ahead.

Fifteen minutes later she was in the lovers' seat in the cool blue room, her wrist exposed, waiting for Alicia Aguado's inquisitive fingers. They talked about the bomb first. Consuelo couldn't concentrate. She was busy trying to hold her fragmentary self together. Talk of the shattering effects of the bomb was not helping.

'You were a little late,' said Alicia, placing her fingers on the pulse. 'Did you come straight here?'

'I was delayed at work. I came as soon as I could get away.'

'No distractions?'

'None.'

'Try answering that question again, Consuelo.'

She stared at her wrist. Was her heartbeat so transparent? She swallowed hard. Why should this be so difficult? She'd had no problem all day. Her eyes filled. A tear slipped to the corner of her mouth.

'Why are you crying, Consuelo?'

'Aren't *you* going to tell *me*?'

'No,' said Aguado, 'it's the other way round. I'm just the guide.'

'I fought a momentary distraction,' said Consuelo.

'Were you reluctant to tell me because it was of a sexual nature?'

'Yes. I'm ashamed of it.'

'Of what exactly?'

No reply.

'Think about that before our next meeting and decide whether it's true,' said Aguado. 'Tell me about the distraction.'

Consuelo related the incident of the previous night, which had finally precipitated her call for help.

'You don't know this man?'

'No.'

'Have you seen him before, had some kind of casual contact?'

'He's one of those types that walks past women and mutters obscenities,' she said. 'I don't tolerate that sort of behaviour and I make a scene whenever it happens. I want to discourage them from doing it to other women.'

'Do you see that as a moral duty?'

'I do. Women should not be subjected to this random sexism. These men should not be encouraged to indulge in their gross fantasies. It has nothing to do with sex, it's purely a power thing, an abuse of power. These men hate women. They want to verbalize their hate. It gives them pleasure to shock and humiliate. If there were women foolish enough to get involved with men like that, they would be physically abused by them. They are wife-beaters in the making.'

'So why are you fascinated by this man?' asked Aguado.

Tears again, which were combined with a strange sense of collapse, of things falling into each other and, just as the gravitational pull of all this inner crumpling seemed to be achieving a terminal velocity, she felt herself untethered, floating away from the person she thought herself to be. It seemed to be an extreme form of a phenomenon she referred to as an existential lurch: a sudden reflective moment, in which the question of what we are doing here on this planet spinning in the void seemed unanswerably huge. Normally it was over in a flash and she was back in the world, but this time it went on and she didn't know whether she was going to be able to get back. She leapt to her feet and held herself together in case she came apart.

'It's all right,' said Alicia, reaching out to her. 'It's all right, Consuelo. You're still here. Come and sit beside me again.'

The chair, the so-called lovers' chair, seemed more like a torturer's seat. A place where instruments would be inserted to reach unbearably painful clusters of nerves and tweak them to previously unexperienced levels of agony.

'I can't do this,' she heard herself saying. 'I can't do it.'

She fell into Alicia Aguado's arms. She needed the

human touch to bring her back. She cried, and the worst of it was that she had no idea what her suffering was about. Alicia got her back into the chair. They sat, fingers intertwined, as if they were now, indeed, lovers.

'I was falling apart,' said Consuelo. 'I lost sight . . . I lost my sense of who I was. I felt like an astronaut, floating away from the mother ship. I was on the brink of madness.'

'And what precipitated that sensation?'

'Your question. I don't remember what it was. Were you asking about a friend, or my father, perhaps?'

'Maybe we've talked enough about what's troubling you,' said Aguado. 'Let's try to end this on a positive note. Tell me something that makes you happy.'

'My children make me happy.'

'If you remember, our last consultation was terminated by a discussion about how your children made you feel. You said . . .'

'I love them so much it hurts,' finished Consuelo.

'Let's think about a state of happiness that's free from pain.'

'I don't feel pain all the time. It's only when I see them sleeping.'

'And how often do you watch them sleeping?'

Consuelo realized that it had become a nightly ritual, watching the boys in their careless sleep was the high point of every day. That pain right in her middle had become something she relished.

'All right,' said Consuelo, carefully, 'let's try to remember a moment of pain-free happiness. That shouldn't be too difficult, should it, Alicia? I mean, here we are in the most beautiful city in Spain. Didn't somebody say: "To whom God loves, He gives a house in Seville"? God's love must come with half a million euros these days. Let me see . . . Do you ask all your patients this question?'

'Not all of them.'

'How many have been able to give you an answer?' asked Consuelo. 'I imagine psychologists meet a lot of *un*happy people.'

'There's always something. People who love the country might think of the way the sunlight plays on water, or the wind in the grasses. City people might think of a painting they've seen, or a ballet, or just sitting in their favourite square.'

'I don't go to the country. I used to like art, but I lost . . .'

'Others remember a friendship, or an old flame.'

Their hands had come apart and Aguado's fingers were back on Consuelo's wrist.

'What are you thinking about now, for instance?' she asked.

'It's nothing,' said Consuelo.

'It's not *nothing*,' said Aguado. 'Whatever it is . . . hold on to it.'

Inés had been sitting in the apartment for over an hour. It was some time after 9.30 p.m. She had tried to call Esteban but, as usual, his mobile was turned off. She was quite calm, although inside her head there seemed to be a wire pulled taut to vibrating point. She had been to see her doctor but had left just before she was due to be called. The doctor would want to examine her and she didn't want to be looked at, pried into.

The incident in the park with the mulatto bitch-whore kept intruding on her internal movie, forcing the film out of the gate and jamming her head with other images: the lividness of Esteban's face as it appeared under the bed and the twitching of his bare feet on the cold kitchen floor.

The kitchen was not a place for her to be. The hard edges of its granite work surfaces, the chill of the marble floor, the distorting mirrors of all the chrome were reminders of the morning's brutality. She hated that fascist kitchen. It made her think of the Guardia Civil in jackboots and their hard, black, shiny hats. She couldn't see a child in that kitchen.

She sat in the bedroom, feeling tiny on the huge and empty marital bed. The TV was off. There was too much talk about the bomb, too many images of the site, too much blood, gore, and shattered glass and lives. She looked at herself in the mirror, over the ordered hairbrushes and cufflink collections. A question danced in her brain: What the fuck has happened to me?

By 9.45 p.m. she couldn't bear it any longer and went outside. She thought she was walking aimlessly, but found herself drawn to the young people already beginning to gather in the warm night under the massive trees of the Plaza del Museo. Then, unaccountably, she was in Calle Bailén and standing in front of her ex-husband's house. The sight of it brought up a spike of envy. She could have had this house, or at least half of it, if it hadn't been for that bitch of a lawyer Javier had hired. It was she who'd found out that Inés had been fucking Esteban Calderón for months and had asked (to her face!) if she'd wanted all that tawdry stuff dragged through the courts. And look at her now. What a great move she'd made. Married to an abuser

236

of women, who, when he wasn't sodomizing his wife, 'for purposes of contraception', was off with every unpaid whore who waggled her tits . . . Where had all this terrible language come from? Inés Conde de Tejada didn't use this sort of language. Why was her mind suddenly so full of filth?

But here she was, outside Javier's house. Her slim legs in her short skirt trembled. She carried on past the doors to the Hotel Colón and turned back. She had to see Javier. She had to tell him. Not that she'd been beaten. Not that she was sorry for what she had done. No, she didn't want to tell him anything. She just wanted to be near a man who had loved her, who had adored her.

As she hid in the darkness of the orange trees and prepared herself, the door opened and three men came out. They went to pick up a taxi outside the Hotel Colón. The door closed. Inés rang the bell. Falcón reopened the door and was stunned to see the oddly diminished figure of his ex-wife.

'Hola, Inés. Are you all right?'

'Hola, Javier.'

They kissed. He made way for her. They walked to the patio with Falcón thinking: She looks as small and thin as a child. He cleared away the remnants of the CNI party and returned with a bottle of manzanilla.

'I should have thought after a day like today you'd be exhausted,' she said. 'And yet here you are having people round for drinks.'

'It's been a long day,' said Falcón, thinking: What is this all about? 'How's Esteban holding up?'

'I haven't seen him.'

'He's probably still at the site. They're working a

237

roster system through the night,' said Falcón. 'Are you all right, Inés?'

'You've asked me that already, Javier. Don't I look all right?'

'You're not worried about anything, are you?'

'Do I look worried?'

'No, just a little thin. Have you lost weight?'

'I keep myself in shape.'

It always bewildered Falcón, who was already running out of things to say to Inés, how he could ever have been obsessed by her. She struck him now as completely banal; an expert in chitchat, a beautiful presenter of received opinion, a snob and a bore. And yet before they married they'd had a passionate affair, with wild sexual encounters. The bronze boy in the fountain had fled from their excesses.

Her heels clicked on the marble flags of the patio. He had wanted to get rid of her as soon as he'd seen her, but there was something about her pitiful frailness, her lack of Sevillana *hauteur*, that made it hard for him to brush her off into the night.

'How's things?' he said, trying to nod something more interesting into his head, which was almost completely taken up with the decision he had to make within the next eight hours. 'How's life with Esteban?'

'You see more of him than I do,' she said.

'We haven't worked together for a while and, you know, he's always been ambitious, so . . .'

'Yes, he's always been ambitious,' she said, 'to fuck every woman that passes under his nose.'

Falcón's glass of manzanilla stopped on its way to his mouth, before continuing. He took a good inch off the top.

'I wouldn't know,' he said, avoiding a conversational line that had been common knowledge in the police and judiciary for years.

'Don't be so fucking ridiculous, Javier,' she said. 'The whole of fucking Seville knows he's been dipping his cock in every pussy that comes his way.'

Silence. Falcón wondered if he'd ever heard Inés use this sort of language before. It was as if some fishwife inside her was kicking down the barriers.

'I came across one of his whores today in the Murillo Gardens,' she said. 'I recognized her from a shot he'd taken of her with his digital camera. And she was sitting in front of me on a park bench, smoking a cigar, as if she was still thinking about sucking his –'

'Come on, Inés,' said Falcón. 'I'm not the person you should be talking to about this.'

'Why not?' she said. 'You know me. We've been intimate. You know him. You know what he's . . . that he's a . . . that I . . .'

She broke down. Falcón took the glass out of her hand, found some tissues. She blew her nose and thumped the tabletop with her fist and tried to dig her heel into the floor of the patio, which made her wince. She took a walk around the fountain and felt a sudden stabbing pain in her side and had to hold on to herself.

'Are you all right, Inés?'

'Stop asking me that question,' she said. 'It's nothing, just some kidney-stone trouble. The doctor says I don't drink enough water.'

He fetched her a glass of water and thought about how he was going to manage this situation, with Mark Flowers due any minute. His brain stalled on the ludicrous fact that *she* had come to see *him* to talk about

239

her husband's incorrigible womanizing. What did that mean?

'I wanted to talk to you,' she said, 'because I have no one else I can talk to. My friends aren't capable of this level of intimacy. I'm sure some of them have become his conquests. My suffering would just be gossip to them, nothing more. I know you went through a very bad time a few years ago and that has given you the capacity to understand what I'm going through now.'

'I'm not sure my experiences are comparable,' said Falcón, frowning at her self-absorbed talk, the situation expanding out of his control by the moment.

'I know that when we split up you were still in love with me,' she said. 'I felt very sorry for you.'

He knew she'd felt nothing of the sort. She'd projected all her guilt on to him and taunted him with that horrific mantra about his heartlessness: '*Tú no tienes corazón, Javier Falcón.*'

'Are you thinking of leaving Esteban?' he asked, carefully, panicked by the notion that she might be thinking that he would have her back.

'*No, no, no que no,*' she said. 'It hasn't come to that. We're made for each other. We've been through so much. I'd never leave him. He needs me. It's just . . .'

It's just that there aren't enough clichés for the cheated wife to draw on, thought Falcón.

'It's just that . . . he needs help,' said Inés.

What was happening today? The CNI wanted him to persuade his new friend to become a spy. His ex-wife wanted him to encourage her husband, with whom he'd only ever had a professional relationship, to go and see a shrink.

'What do you think, Javier?'

'I think it's none of my business,' he said firmly.

'I still want to know what you think,' she said, her eyes huge in her head.

'You'll never persuade Esteban – or any man, for that matter – to go to a shrink or a marriage-guidance counsellor, unless he himself perceives that there is a problem,' said Falcón. 'And most men, in these situations, rarely see that the problem is theirs.'

'He's been whoring around in this marriage since . . . since *before* we got married,' she said. 'He must see that he needs to change.'

'The only thing that will change him is a major trauma in his life, which might make him reflect on his . . . insatiable needs,' said Falcón. 'Unfortunately, it might also mean that those close to him now will not remain so . . .'

'I stuck with him through his last crisis with the American bitch and I'll stick with him through this,' she said. 'I know he loves me.'

'That was my experience,' said Falcón, holding out his hands and realizing that he'd just told Inés why she wasn't a part of his life any more. 'My problem didn't happen to be womanizing, though.'

'No, it wasn't, was it? You were so *cold*, Javier,' she said.

That tone of false concern set his teeth on edge, but the doorbell rang, saving him from having to dig deeper into his reserves of patience. He walked her to the door.

'You're popular tonight,' said Inés.

'I don't know what people see in me,' said Falcón, braking hard on the irony.

'We don't see so much of each other these days,'

241

she said, kissing him before he opened the door. 'I'm sorry . . . if we don't see each other again . . .'

'Again?' said Falcón, and the doorbell rang once more.

'I'm sorry,' she said.

At 9.30 p.m. Calderón had arrived at Marisa's apartment. Twenty minutes later they lay naked and sex-smeared on the floor by the sofa. They were drinking Cuba Libres chock full of ice, and smoking their way through a packet of Marlboro Lights. She straddled him and brushed her hardened nipples against his lips, while lowering her pubis until it just tickled the tip of his exhausted penis. He filled his hands with her buttocks and bit her nipple a little too hard.

'Ai!' she yelped, pushing away from him. 'Haven't you eaten?'

'There hasn't been much time for eating,' he said.

'Why don't I make you some pasta?' she said, standing over him, still in her heels, legs astride, hands on hips, cigarette dangling from her plump lips.

I'm Helmut Newton, thought Calderón.

'Sounds good,' he said.

She put on a turquoise silk robe and went into the kitchen. Calderón sipped his drink, smoked, looked out into the dense, warm night, and thought: This is all right.

'Something strange happened to me today,' said Marisa, from the kitchen, knife working over some onion and garlic. 'I sold a couple of my pieces to one of my dealers. He pays cash and I like to treat myself to a nice cigar – a real one, made in Havana. I sit under the palm trees in the Murillo Gardens to smoke it, because it reminds me of home and it was really hot today, the first heat of the summer. And I'd just got myself into a really cool Cuban mood . . .'

Marisa could tell from the back of Calderón's head that he was barely listening to her.

'. . . when this woman sat down in front of me. A beautiful woman. Very slim, long dark hair, beautiful big eyes . . . Maybe a little too thin, now that I think about it. Her eyes were *so* big and she was staring at me in this *very* strange way.'

She had his attention now. His head was as still as rock.

'I like to smoke my cigars in peace. I don't like mad people looking at me. So I asked her what she was staring at. She told me she was looking at the whore with the cigar – *la puta con el puro*. Well, nobody calls me a whore, and nobody ruins a top-quality Havana cigar. So I gave her a piece of my mind – and you know what?'

Calderón took a viciously long drag of his cigarette.

'You know what she said to me?'

'What?' said Calderón, as if a long way off.

'She said: "You're the *whore* who's fucking my husband." She asked me how much you were paying me and said that it didn't look as if it was more than € 15 a night and that you'd probably thrown in the copper wig and the cigar to keep me happy. Can you tell me how the fuck Inés knows who I am?'

Calderón stood up. He was so angry he couldn't speak. His lips were pale and his genitals were shrivelled back into their pubic nest as if his rage had taken all available blood to keep it stoked. He was clenching and unclenching his fist and staring off into the night, with bone-snapping violence ricocheting around his head. Marisa had seen this trait in physically un-impressive men before. The big, muscly guys had nothing to prove, whereas the fat, the puny and the stupid had big lessons to hand out.

When she heard the shower running, Marisa stopped preparing the food. Calderón dressed in ominous silence. She asked him what he was doing, why he was leaving. He whipped his tie up into a tight chol-eric knot.

'Nobody talks to you like that,' he said, and left.

Inés stopped to look in a hand-painted tile shop on Calle Bailén. She felt better after seeing Javier. She'd persuaded herself, in the short walk after their brief encounter, that Javier still cared for her. How sweet of him to ask her if she was thinking of leaving Esteban. He still lived in hope after all these years. It was sad to have to disappoint him.

The darkness under the huge trees of the Plaza del Museo held the murmur of more young people, the chinking of beer bottles and the reek of marijuana. She walked through them feeling more cheerful. The light was on in the apartment, which elated her. Esteban was home. He had come back to her. They were going to repair the damage. She was sure, after what had happened this morning, that he would see reason and she could persuade him to make an appointment with a psychologist.

The stairs no longer inspired dread and although the pain in her side meant that she didn't exactly sprint up them, she reached the door with a lightness of heart. Her hair swung on her shoulders as she closed the door.

She instantly felt his looming presence. A smile was already spreading on her face when he sheafed her hair and turned it once around his wrist. She toppled backwards, falling to her knees, and he brought her face up close to the pallor of the pure hatred in his own.

18

Mark Flowers had already eaten. His American digestive system had never got used to the Spanish custom of not even thinking about dinner until 9.30 p.m. He turned down Falcón's offers of beer and manzanilla and opted for a single malt whisky. Falcón wolfed down a quickly made sandwich in the kitchen and stuck with the manzanilla. It was still very warm and they sat out under the open sky of the patio.

'So what did "your own" people want to talk to you about?' asked Flowers, always a man to get his questions in first.

'They're trying to persuade me to go into the recruitment business for them.'

'And will you do it?'

'I've got until 6 a.m. to decide.'

'Well, it was nice of them to wait until you had nothing on your plate,' said Flowers, who was always determined to show him that not all Americans had undergone an irony bypass. 'I don't know who they want you to recruit, but if he's a friend he might not stay a friend. That's the way these things work, in my experience.'